RETURN TO
Rockytop

BY JEAN CAMPION

WESTERN REFLE

Kay Zillich

ISBN: 978-1-932738-53-7

First Edition
Printed in the United States of America

Cover painting and map by Catherine Dougharty

Western Reflections Publishing Company®
P.O. Box 1149
Lake City, CO 81235
www.westernreflectionspub.com

*Not to know what happened before we were born
is to be perpetually a child.
For what is the worth of a human life
unless it is woven into the life of our ancestors?*
— *Cicero*

*To forget one's ancestors is to be
a brook without a source,
or a tree without a root.*
— *Chinese Proverb*

Dedication

꒰꒱

This book is dedicated to all Teachers: past, present, and future.
You have the hardest job in the world. And the best.
And the most important.
Carry on.

Acknowledgments

I would like to thank the members of the following organizations for their help in the process of writing and editing this book: Word Wranglers, Southwest Christian Writers, and Western Reflections Publishing. In addition, Chris Goold, Jenny Coons, Catherine Dougharty, and Tom Campion provided valuable assistance.

I also thank my ancestors for having the foresight and fortitude to come west in covered wagons. And I remember those ancestors who passed on the legacy of teaching: John Benjamin Griffith, David Dale Griffith, Florence Kitelely Griffith, Eleanor Griffith Ferguson, Ed Griffith, Lillian Griffith Carpenter.

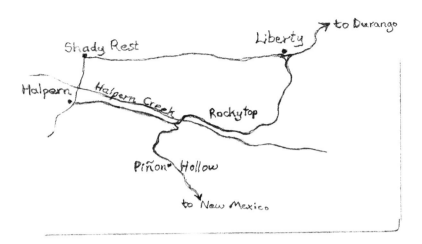

Shady Rest Liberty to Durango

Halpern Halpern Creek Rockytop

Piñon Hollow

to New Mexico

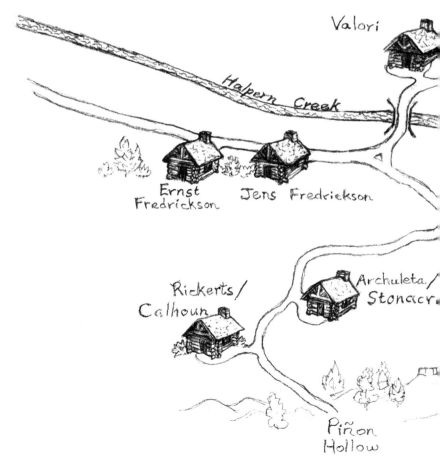

Valori

Halpern Creek

Ernst Fredrickson Jens Fredrickson

Rickerts/ Calhoun Archuleta/ Stonacr...

Piñon Hollow

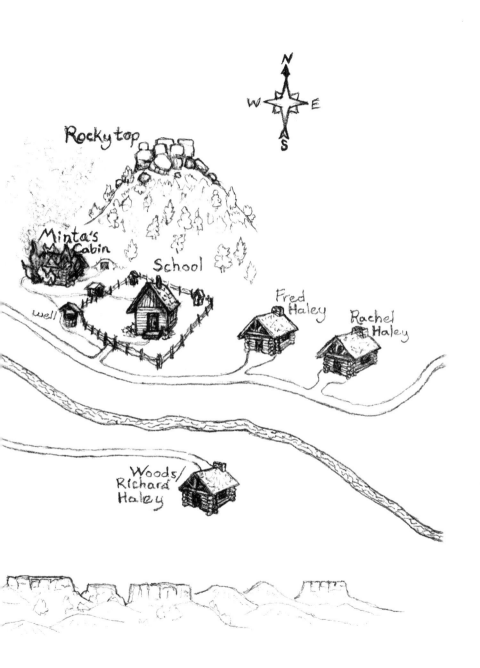

Rockytop Residents, 1920-1921

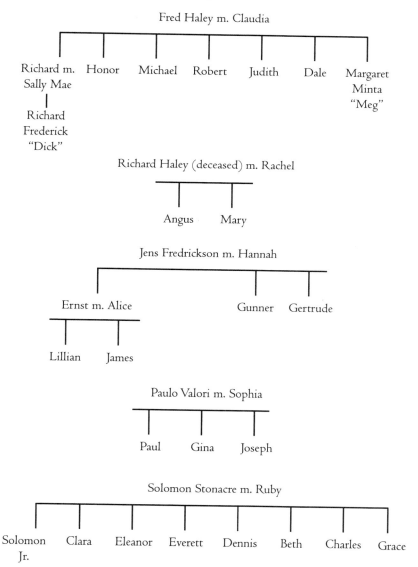

Fred Haley m. Claudia

Richard m. Sally Mae | Honor | Michael | Robert | Judith | Dale | Margaret Minta "Meg"

Richard Frederick "Dick"

Richard Haley (deceased) m. Rachel

Angus | Mary

Jens Fredrickson m. Hannah

Ernst m. Alice | Gunner | Gertrude

Lillian | James

Paulo Valori m. Sophia

Paul | Gina | Joseph

Solomon Stonacre m. Ruby

Solomon Jr. | Clara | Eleanor | Everett | Dennis | Beth | Charles | Grace

Clayton "Silas" Calhoun/Algernon Rickerts

Minta Mayfield

The Little School House

Mud and straw and cedar posts
Protected from the wind.
Sod and bark upon the roof
Kept rain from getting in.

Children rode on horse or mule
Or walked four miles or more
To reach the little school house
And enter by the door.

The stove that sat inside
Provided more than heat.
It warmed up soup for lunches,
Dried shoes and socks for feet.

The teacher carried water
And brought the fire wood in.
She swept and scrubbed the floor
So the school day could begin.

Reading, writing, arithmetic,
History, geography, too,
Orthography and penmanship,
Lots for one teacher to do.

School was very important
To our ancestors long ago.
They endured hardships
That we today forgo.

Then bigger schools were built.
Buses took the kids away.
The little school was left alone
To crumble and decay.

If I could have that school house back,
I'd invite you to come inside
To learn what it could teach us
About American values and pride.

by Jean Campion

CHAPTER ONE

Lulabelle's Secret

 srjekv

Monday, August 23, 1920, Liberty Colorado—*Today is the day I've been waiting for all summer. I will be reunited with cousin Lulabelle at long last and can begin to try to make up to her for all the suffering she has had to endure because of me. Everyone says that it was not my fault, that I could not control Edmund, but if I had not fled from him and our marriage, none of the rest would have occurred. Of course, I would be dead, but maybe that would have been for the best. At least, then, he wouldn't have attacked Frank and Lulabelle to make them tell him where I was.*

"You can't turn back time, Ellie," Grandmother was fond of telling me. Never have I found her words more true or more painful. I wonder what she would think of my new name—Minta Mayfield—and my new surroundings—the mountains of southwest Colorado? I miss her so much. At least I now have the Posts, Miriam, who has become very dear to me this summer, and her husband, Matthew, my wise mentor. They are about the same age as my parents, who were in their forties when I was born—more like grandparents than parents.

And I'm returning to Rockytop! When I left there last spring, I was afraid I'd never see the Halpern Valley or my students again. After Edmund tried to kill me, burned the teacherage, and attempted to burn the school, I thought they wouldn't want me as their teacher any more. They said they did but couldn't afford to rebuild the teacherage. I didn't want to board with a family—not after finally gaining my independence from Edmund. It seemed an impossible situation. But when I found out they were building an addition onto the school for a teacher's bedroom, I began to reconsider. Finally, I followed my heart instead of my head and agreed to return.

Now, if only I could be sure Edmund perished when he jumped off the train in Missouri last spring, as Sheriff Upton seems to believe, all would be well. As it is, I'm always looking over my shoulder, expecting to see him again. They said he couldn't have survived the injuries he must have received, but I, better than anyone, know the extent of his will. Why didn't they find his body? The authorities were quick to decide it had been washed downstream and stopped looking for him. I would never have stopped— just as he will never stop looking for me, if he's alive.

Minta put down her pen. Her diary entries so often seemed to return to Edmund even when she tried to avoid thinking or writing about him. Sometimes the only thing to do was stop and do something else. She looked out the window at the hustle and bustle on the busy streets of Liberty, Colorado. It was a town growing at an alarming rate. New buildings were being built on nearly every block, and the traffic from motor vehicles and wagons was almost constant as soon as the sun rose. The opening of the new coal mine had revived the former gold and silver mining town and reanimated its once sleepy streets.

Minta's cousin, Lulabelle, and her husband, Frank Jackson, were coming to Liberty to start up a dry goods store. And, of course, to start a new life away from Indiana and Edmund's nearly fatal attack on them. Minta had come here to start a new life, so it was fitting that they would, too. Lulabelle, her more-than-cousin, had been her constant companion growing up. Closer than sisters, they had shared everything. How ironic that they had also shared Edmund's violence.

Minta paced nervously in the Post's small upstairs bedroom. She wanted to see Lulabelle but was nervous about in what condition she might find her. Frank's letters had been reassuring on the surface, but Minta could tell there was more he was not telling her. Most of her information came from the sheriff, who passed on what he learned from the law in Indiana after Edmund was captured, and arrangements were being made to send him back to face trial for the attempted murders of Frank and Lulabelle. Minta suspected that Mo, Sheriff Upton, didn't tell her all the gory details. What he told her was bad enough—

how Edmund had gagged Lulabelle, tied her to the bed, and waited for Frank to come home. Then he'd threatened to—Mo said—"mistreat" Lulabelle if Frank didn't disclose Minta's location. After getting all the information he could, he battered them both with his gun and left them to die. At least he hadn't shot them, probably because the neighbors would hear. Fortunately some friends of Frank's came over and found them before they lay there too long.

Lulabelle hadn't written to Minta at all after the attack. She had to be retaught to feed herself, to walk, and to read. Perhaps she couldn't write. If that were the case, Minta would teach her. But maybe Lulabelle blamed Minta for what happened, as she had every right to do. Minta would have to work hard to regain her trust and love.

A discrete knock on the door told Minta that Miriam was ready for their daily walk to the post office. Matthew had already left with the wagon to pick up Frank and Lulabelle and their belongings at the train station in Durango. Minta hadn't gone along so as to leave more room for them.

She wiped the pen dry and closed her diary. She set it with her Bible on the bedside table ready to continue her daily devotions and writing when she returned. When she was as anxious as she was today, Bible reading and writing in her diary calmed her nerves. Just this morning God had spoken to her in Galatians 5:1: *Stand fast therefore in the liberty wherewith Christ hath made us free, and be not entangled again with the yoke of bondage.* She had been in bondage to Edmund, but now she was beginning to feel free, here in Liberty.

A cloud of dust drew her attention back to the street. A rickety wagon stopped in front of the hardware store, and a man and teenaged boy jumped down. The boy was almost as tall and broad shouldered as the man. They had the same straw-like hair, and she knew they must be two of the Stonacres. The local grapevine said Sol Stonacre and his family had moved into the Archuleta place near Silas Calhoun's ranch by Piñon Hollow. There were eight Stonacre children and a wisp of a mother who had been seen in town only once. Everyone from the

Halpern Valley did their shopping in Liberty and were well-known to the locals.

Minta hadn't paid much attention to the talk about the Stonacres until Matthew Post said the children, the ones who were old enough, would be attending Rockytop School because Piñon Hollow School was closed. Claire Carpenter, the former school mistress, had married a rancher from Aztec, New Mexico, taken her brood, and moved on. There was no longer a teacher there, nor enough students for a school. There would only be three schools in the Halpern Valley district now: Rockytop, Halpern, and Shady Rest. As Liberty and Durango grew, the population out around Rockytop Mountain seemed to shrink. It was hard to support a family there with water in Halpern Creek only part of the year and crops dependent on the undependable weather. The farmers who stuck it out were the best ones, those who didn't mind doing without.

Minta knew she couldn't expect things to stay the same, but she would miss the Archuleta girls as well as Florence and Wendell Woods who had all moved to Durango. How would these new Stonacre children fit in at school? Last year everyone had been new to her. This year only the Stonacres would, so her job should be much easier. She smiled as she thought of getting back to Rockytop, tidying up the little one-room schoolhouse, wiping the boards clean, and writing the new names there along with those of the returning students. She pictured the Haley and Valori kids' faces along with the Fredrickson twins'. Some she saw in town over the summer, but others she'd not run into. It would be fun to see how much they'd grown and matured. Right now the new Stonacre children were just names to her. Soon they would be real children, real challenges.

Another knock reminded her that Miriam was waiting. She would miss Miriam when she returned to Rockytop but looked forward to being back near Claudia Haley, her closest friend in the Halpern Valley.

Minta put on her hat and opened the door. Miriam stood ready to go to town with her gloves on and her gray hair neatly pinned up under her hat. She was one of those women who aged beautifully, the years making her face look wise and kind rather than old.

"Ready to go, dear?" Miriam asked. "I'll bet you're anxious to see your kinfolks."

"Oh, yes," Minta said as they started downstairs. "And I'm looking forward to your meeting Lulabelle."

"And I, her," Miriam said. "You've told me so much about her that I feel I know her already. Are you still worried about her . . . health?"

"Yes. I know she's not fully recovered. It pains me to think about how she might be—scarred—inside and out. I know she suffered severe head injuries when Edmund hit both her and Frank with his gun, but I don't know any of the details."

As they began to cross the street, Miriam started to reassure Minta. "They must be recovering very well to be able to move to . . ."

Suddenly a wagon pulled into the street behind them. The driver shouted, urging the horse into a fast trot, covering the two ladies with dust as the wagon rumbled by them, its springs complaining loudly.

Minta squeezed her eyes shut until the dust settled and then coughed. "How rude!" Most people drove slowly and carefully on Liberty's Main Street. "We could have been run over! And now there's dust all over my clean dress. Who was that?"

"That, my dear, was Sol Stonacre. I'm sure you've heard Matthew speak of him. He's new around here. Perhaps he'll learn some manners soon."

"I certainly hope so. And I guess I'll be trying to teach some to his children. Hopefully they'll take after their mother instead of him."

Miriam chuckled. "If anyone can teach them some manners, it's you, dear. They don't stand a chance of resisting your kind and patient teaching. You know, I think God puts people in certain places at certain times for a reason. He put you here to save you from Edmund. Now He's put the Stonacres here to . . ."

"To what?" Minta asked. "Save them from themselves?"

"Maybe so, dear, maybe so."

Outwardly Lulabelle looked almost the same—a little thinner, a few lines around her mouth and eyes that hadn't been there before, but no visible scars. Her blond curls were as unruly as ever and her blue eyes as big and open as ever. But something was different. Her greeting hug had been brief, not like the exuberant hugs and screams and kisses with which she had always greeted Minta in the past. Minta smiled when she remembered the disgust Edmund had always shown toward Lulabelle's enthusiasm. Even Edmund's sour countenance hadn't silenced Lulabelle. But, then, she guessed, in the end he had. First he had kept her and Lulabelle apart. Then he had . . .

Minta studied Lulabelle whenever she had a minute between helping unload the wagon and setting things to rights in the the small apartment above what was to be the dry goods store. At Frank and Minta's insistence, Lulabelle stayed upstairs while the others fetched and carried. She busied herself putting dishes and linens away and making a pot of tea for the workers. Whenever she caught Minta staring at her, she turned away. Finally she sat down on a kitchen chair at the small table and simply directed Minta where to put things. Frank had warned Minta that Lulabelle tired easily.

After the work was done, the tea finished, and polite words exchanged, Miriam took her leave to let Minta and Lulabelle be alone. Frank went off with Matthew to get a load of lumber for building shelves downstairs for the soon-to-arrive merchandise.

"Just leave these dishes," Minta said. "I'll wash them up later."

"I'm not an in . . . in . . . I can wash dishes," Lulabelle protested. She set her teacup down on the table with such force Minta was afraid it would crack. "Sometimes I can't remember the word I want. It's so frustrating!"

"I know you're not an invalid, but Frank said you need a lot of rest. How are you, Lulabelle, really?" Minta asked. "Besides the memory loss Frank told me about. I've been so fearful about your condition."

Lulabelle laughed, but not the girlish laugh Minta remembered. This laugh carried a hint of animosity. "My condition? Didn't you notice my condition?"

"Lulabelle, what? I don't understand. Of course, I know you're still recovering. You're doing very well. Frank told me the doctor said you'll gradually get your memory back and be able to remember more words."

"No, Ella Jane. I mean M . . .M . . . Minta? See? I can't even remember your new name. *This* condition." Lulabelle stood, turned her profile to Minta, and pulled her dress tight against her body.

Minta gasped. "Why Lulabelle! You're with child! Why didn't you write me? Or have Frank do it? How wonderful! I know how you and Frank have been wanting a child. When is it due?"

"Mid-January, I think. I'm about four months along."

"My friend Claudia is expecting late this fall. I can't wait for you two to meet. Two babies!" Minta smiled, thinking of being able to enjoy two new little ones soon. Lulabelle wasn't smiling. "What is it Lulabelle? You don't look very happy."

Lulabelle twirled a piece of her hair around one finger the way she used to when they were kids and something was bothering her. She avoided looking at Minta as she answered. "I used to think being with . . . with child would make me happy. I know better now."

"Why aren't you happy? Aren't you well? Isn't the baby well?"

"The doctor says I'm fine; the baby's fine."

"Then what is it? Lulabelle, I know you too well. What's wrong? Isn't Frank happy about the baby?"

"Frank is es . . . es . . . happy." Lulabelle sat suddenly in the chair and folded her arms on the table, letting her head drop onto them, sobbing. "I haven't told Frank what's wrong. I've told no one. I'm not even sure I can tell you."

"What do you mean? Surely Frank knows all about your condition. You said you'd been to a doctor." Minta pulled her chair closer to Lulabelle, stroking her hair as she'd done when they were girls and Lulabelle lay in bed with the flu. "You know you can tell me anything,

Lulabelle. We've never had secrets. You were the only one I could tell all—well, most of—the things Edmund did to me. I love you."

Lulabelle continued to sob, but gradually the sobs diminished and finally stopped. "Now, what is it?" Minta asked.

"I'm afraid," Lulabelle whispered. "Afraid of . . . of when the baby comes."

"You're afraid of childbirth? That's natural. I'm sure everyone is the first time, but my friend Claudia says there's nothing to fear. She's expecting her seventh child. I'll arrange for you to meet her soon and . . ."

"I'm afraid I won't be able to love it." Lulabelle stared at Minta with blank, fixed eyes.

"Not love your own baby? Lulabelle! I don't understand."

"If I tell you, you must promise on . . . on Grandmother's grave that you won't tell another living soul. Es . . . es . . . especially Frank."

"Lulabelle! You shouldn't have secrets from Frank. Whatever it is, I'm sure he'd understand."

"Promise me!" Lulabelle reached out and gripped Minta's hand so hard she thought the bones would be crushed.

"All right," Minta said. "I promise on Grandmother's grave I won't tell another living soul." She waited. The silence in the room was broken only by an occasional sob from Lulabelle.

Minta took a clean handkerchief out of her apron pocket and offered it to her cousin.

Lulabelle sat up straight and blew her nose. "Don't look at me while I tell you," she said.

Minta turned her chair and stared out the window. "Tell me."

"I'm afraid the baby isn't Frank's. I'm afraid it's . . . it's Edmund's."

Minta felt the room spin. She gripped the edge of the table, glad she wasn't standing up. "I thought Edmund only gave you a concussion and some bruises. Are you saying he . . . he . . . forced himself . . ." Minta's voice broke and she couldn't go on. The dingy gray wall in front of her looked red, like blood.

"Yes," Lulabelle whispered. "I didn't remember at first. When the

. . . m . . . m . . . memories first started to come back, I thought they were just bad dreams. But now I remember all he did and said. He knocked on the door and yelled, 'Telegram for Mrs. Jackson!' I was so stupid, I opened the door. Then I tried not to let him in, but he pushed his way past me like I was made of f . . . f . . . feathers. He was laughing. He was there, in the house, a long time before Frank came home. He tied me to the bed, and he said I owed him since you deprived him of his . . . his. . . rights. And then he . . . I can't say it."

"You don't need to. I, more than anyone, know what he's capable of." Minta's fingernails were biting into her palms as she clenched her fists. She wanted to run screaming from the room, but she had to let Lulabelle tell her story. It had been bottled up too long.

"By the time Frank got home, Edmund had covered me back up and tied a kitchen towel around my mouth so I couldn't call out to him. When Edmund threatened to . . . to . . . hurt me, I couldn't tell Frank he already had. Frank told him what he wanted to know then. I'm so sorry. That's how Edmund found you."

"Of course Frank had to tell him. I never meant to put either of you in danger. But why didn't you tell Frank or the law or the doctor what Edmund did to you? Why have you kept it a secret?"

"The next part is the only part I still don't remember. That must be when Edmund hit us both in the head and left us to die. If some friends of Frank's hadn't stopped by, we would have died. By the time I remembered what happened, it was too late for a doctor to do anything. The law had found Edmund and then lost him again. Frank was already crazy with rage. He would have gone off to hunt Edmund down and kill him. I needed him to stay with me. But now he's so happy about the baby. I can't tell him now. What if the baby looks like Edmund? Oh, Minta, I couldn't bear it—to have a daily re. . . re. . . reminder of what he did to me."

Minta turned back to Lulabelle and took both her hands in hers, gently. "Lulabelle, listen to me. The baby is not Edmund's. I know. Let me tell you a story that Edmund's doctor told to me."

She told Lulabelle about the conversation she'd had with the doctor back in Indiana who had attributed Minta's barrenness to Edmund's bout of mumps as a teenager. "So you see, Lulabelle, he can't father children."

Lulabelle looked up hopefully. "Are you sure? Did the doctor say it was completely im . . . im . . . impossible?"

Minta hesitated.

"He didn't, did he?" Lulabelle asked. "Don't lie to me. Not about this. It's too important."

"He said it was '*extremely* unlikely.'"

"Unlikely, but not impossible?"

"Well, yes, I suppose."

"So I'm back where we started. What if the baby is born black-haired instead of sandy like Frank? I know I won't be able to love it."

"Claudia says all her babies are born with black hair. She says they all look like little Indians when they're born. And now they're the fairest-haired bunch of kids you'll ever see."

"But what if . . ."

"Lulabelle, stop! Grandmother always said you used to 'what if' her to death. You will love this baby because it's yours. Even if the father is Edmund, which, as I said, is almost impossible. If I had had a child by Edmund, I would have loved it, even though I hated Edmund. It's not the child that's at fault. Babies aren't born bad. Even Edmund wasn't. His brother said he got that way because of how his father treated him after their mother died. You will love this child. And Frank will love it. And I will. And it will grow up to be happy and good and strong."

"Oh, Minta. I hope you're right. I hope the baby is born early. That will mean it's Frank's. We weren't together . . . that way . . . for a long time after . . . after Edmund attacked us. So if it's Frank's, I had to have already been with child then. I hope it comes early."

"I do, too. I hope it's early and has sandy hair and Frank's big chin with whiskers growing on it already. Then you'll stop all this foolishness."

Lulabelle laughed—her old laugh—the one Minta remembered.

"You always could talk me into, or out of, anything, Minta. I guess that's why you became a teacher. So you could keep telling people what to do."

CHAPTER TWO

Sari's Secret

❦

Devil's Creek Missouri, August 1920

Sari stood on the porch steps and watched her son Orville and her new man Eddie out in the field. The old mule they had hitched to the plow hadn't been worked much lately, and they were having a rough time. Eddie was impatient. He raised his hand and cuffed Orville on the ear. She wished he wouldn't be so hard on the boy. True, Orville tended to be lazy, but since his pa died, he hadn't had anyone to teach him how to do things around the place. Not that her man had been that great of a worker, either.

Her man. She'd have to quit thinking of him like that. Eddie was her man now. She hadn't intended it to happen. She thought she'd nurse him back to health and get some work out of him before he moved on. But somewhere in the days of taking care of his body, she'd started to desire that body. When she changed and bathed him and saw the male stirrings, old longings she'd thought had been left far behind came to the surface.

It wasn't a conscious decision. One day she just lifted her skirts and climbed on top of him there on the bed. His eyes widened in surprise, but he didn't try to stop her. In fact, he reached for her with both hands and gripped her so tightly he left bruises on her thighs. Even his rough hands felt good to her. It became a regular part of her routine of caring for him. And when he was up and around, it didn't stop. It intensified.

Now she and Eddie lived together as man and wife. She knew she wanted that to continue and that she wanted to have more children. Orville, the only one of her four to survive, was almost of the age to go off on his own. He didn't need her no more. Two boys had been born dead, and her poor little Betsy Belle died of pneumonia when she was two. That had been almost more than she could bear. If she hadn't had her man and Orville to take care of, there'd have been no use going on. After the feud with the neighbors that left her man dead, she and Orville cut themselves off from contact with people, except for going to town to sell eggs and buy necessities. Now she had another chance at more children. If nothing else, Eddie would be good for that. She'd have to figure out how to keep him here.

Eddie headed back toward the house, leaving Orville struggling with the uncooperative mule. Eddie's limp was getting better, but he still used a stick to walk. At first she'd been afraid he'd never walk again, but by sheer determination he forced himself up on the leg she had set, gritted his teeth, and taught himself to walk with the stick. A less stubborn man would have stayed in bed and allowed her to take care of him. His nose healed up crooked, while the scar on his left cheek remained thick and red. His hair had gone all gray during his convalescence, and the beard he was growing was coming in gray as well. She'd kept him clean-shaven when she cared for him, but as soon as he was up on his own, he decided to grow a beard.

"It makes you look ten years older, Eddie," she said one day. "I hardly recognize you as the man we pulled out of the river that day."

"Good," he replied.

She didn't ask for an explanation. She knew better. Eddie told you what he wanted, when he wanted, and you'd better not press him in the meantime. You'd expect anyone living with the pain he had to be cranky, but she suspected Eddie had been born that way. Crankiness was as much a part of him as the muscles in his arms and shoulders that seemed to grow each day as he walked around more and more with his stick. She was getting used to his bad temper. And getting used to doing what she had to do so as not to provoke him.

"That boy of yours is about as dumb as a tree stump," Eddie said when he reached the porch.

"Uh, huh," Sari replied. She knew sticking up for Orville would only make Eddie's treatment of him worse. "You're doing a good job of fixing up this old place, Eddie. We shore thank you for that," she said.

"Well, it needs a lot of fixing, that's sure as sure. Never saw such a run-down heap. Thought I'd landed in hillbilly heaven when I woke up."

Sari giggled. "You shore did. You know I ain't a educated woman, Eddie, but . . ."

"Humph! Had me about enough of educated women. Too smart for their own good, you ask me." He turned his head slightly and spit, barely missing her shoe.

"Eddie, I been thinking. Ain't it 'bout time you made a honest woman of me? I mean, any day now I might be, you know, in the family way. We ought to go into town to the justice of the peace and . . ."

"Now that would be a great idea. If I was free to marry, which I ain't." His black eyes bored into her.

"What do you mean you ain't free to marry? You mean just 'cause you don't remember much about where you come from or who you is?"

"No. I remember enough to know I'm already married. But I've been thinking, too. That could be fixed."

"Fixed? How?" Sari asked, her eyes filling with tears. If Eddie knew he was already married, why did he so willingly share her bed? And why hadn't he ever said anything about going home? Wherever that was.

"When it's time for you to know that, I'll tell you," Eddie said. "In the meantime, I'll be ready for dinner in about half an hour. It better be ready for me." He turned and limped toward the barn.

"Yes, Eddie," Sari said, turning to go back into the kitchen. "It'll be ready." She knew Eddie would be in a foul mood if dinner wasn't ready and to his liking on time. It was funny how quickly she'd learned what he wanted and how to give it to him. She was a strong woman, but, even injured, he was stronger. When they fought, she tried to give as good as she got, but it was easiest to give in. The first time she hit him back, he looked startled, then laughed. Then he hit her again, harder. As he recovered from his injuries and his strength returned, she knew who would always come out on the losing end of a physical fight—especially since he was as apt to use the walking stick for a weapon as not. She'd have to figure out some other way to handle him.

CHAPTER THREE

Back to School

⌘⌘⌘

Tuesday, August 31, 1920, Rockytop—*School starts tomorrow. I've only one day to prepare. I remember last year I took a week to get ready. This year I wanted to spend as much time in town with Lulabelle as possible. I'm very worried about her mental state. She tries to put on a brave face, but I know what Edmund did to her is eating her up inside. It's hard for me not to have sinful thoughts about what I'd like to do to Edmund. It almost makes me wish he would come back, so I could kill him. Isn't that terrible? I wouldn't tell these thoughts to anyone but you, dear diary. Hate is such a powerful emotion. It's eating me up inside, too. I so wish they'd find his body and maybe we could all put the past to rest.*

Enough of that! It is good to be back at Rockytop. After the isolation of Edmund's farm and the peace and quiet of Rockytop, it was very hard living in the noise and dust and commotion of Liberty all summer. I much prefer my little room here with the wide open spaces outside. The bedroom the men added onto the school is small but fine for me. It has little windows on the east and west. I will have to cook on the school stove, which doesn't have an oven, and leave the door between my room and the schoolroom open to get heat, but I'll make do. I'm so grateful they did this for me. Frank said they must have really wanted me back to go to all that trouble, but I think they're just planning for the future. Someday Rockytop might have enough students to be a two-room school. Speaking of students, I'd better get busy.

Minta put her diary back on her bedside table and went through the doorway into the schoolroom. She had cleaned it yesterday when she arrived, so all she had to do today was prepare for the first day of school.

She took a piece of chalk and printed the children's names and grades on the board behind her desk to remind her what she needed to plan:

ROCKYTOP SCHOOL, 1920-21

HALEY, ANGUS	8TH GRADE
HALEY, MICHAEL	7TH GRADE
STONACRE, SOLOMON JR.	7TH GRADE
STONACRE, CLARA	7TH GRADE
HALEY, MARY	6TH GRADE
FREDRICKSON, GERTRUDE	5TH GRADE
FREDRICKSON, GUNNER	5TH GRADE
HALEY, ROBERT	5TH GRADE
STONACRE, ELEANOR	4TH GRADE
VALORI, PAUL	4TH GRADE
HALEY, JUDITH	3RD GRADE
STONACRE, EVERETT	3RD GRADE
HALEY, DALE	2ND GRADE
STONACRE, DENNIS	2ND GRADE
STONACRE, BETH	1ST GRADE
VALORI, GINA	1ST GRADE

She stood back and studied the list. Last year she had had fourteen children, half of them grade three and below. This year there were sixteen, but more in the upper grades. That had some advantages and disadvantages. There would be more older ones to help the younger ones with their reading. Their softball team would be much better with older, stronger players. On the other hand, the Stonacre children were behind in school. According to Matthew Post, who had collected all the school records he could find for them, they hadn't attended regularly in the past. Sol was fourteen, Clara thirteen, and the others eleven, nine, eight, and six. Only little Beth would be in the right grade for her age, having just started school. It would be a challenge to get them caught up without causing too much disruption to the other students. Last year, four-year-old Gina had been in first grade, but slept through much of it and didn't complete all the first grade requirements. Minta had decided to keep her in first grade again this year. She was still a year younger than Beth, the other first grader.

It was nice that all the grades except sixth and eighth had more than one student. Minta had found out last year that the students did better when they could work with someone else on their lessons. And the only sixth grader, Mary, would probably be the best student this year. She would do fine by herself. In fact, she might skip up to seventh before the year was out.

The Stonacres were definitely the wild card this year. Time would tell how they would fit in. Minta was a little worried about Angus Haley. He was used to being the oldest and biggest. How would he get along with Solly? Would Solly have a problem with Angus being a grade higher, although younger by a few months? And would Mary be upset about another older girl taking over her role as mother hen to the little ones?

"So much to worry about," Minta said to herself. Then she laughed. "I'm doing just what Grandmother warned against—borrowing trouble from tomorrow when I should be working on today," she said aloud. "Time to get down to work." She often talked aloud to herself when she was alone in the school. It helped to practice her projection—her "teacher voice" as the kids called it.

A soft purr answered her, and she felt Blackie rubbing against her leg. The Valoris had kept the cat all summer and returned her this morning. They said she was used to being outside most of the time now. Minta reached down and rubbed her head. She'd have to let her out soon and see if she would stay around or return to the Valoris' place. She enjoyed the cat's company and her help with mouse control.

She opened her new, green Teacher's Register and copied the names and grades from the board into it. She looked at the blank pages—what would be written there by the end of the year? She picked up last year's red register and thumbed through it. All the attendance information was marked with neat X's. In the back was all the other information she'd had to fill out. The monthly averages for attendance had been very good last year. Only the older boys missed school when there was farm work to be done. There hadn't been much sickness. There was a two in the box asking how many times she'd used corporal punishment. That had been on the same day—Robert and then Angus. None of the children had given her any trouble after that. She hoped she wouldn't have to use the wooden ferule much this year.

Her first year of teaching last year had been a real learning experience. She was lucky she'd had a small group and mostly cooperative students. Once she figured out how to balance all the different grades and lessons and keep everyone busy, the school days went much more smoothly. She closed her eyes and visualized the school as it had been last year—filled with happy, laughing students, the constant hum of their activities a pleasant backdrop to her days. She knew she'd been very lucky to land in such a congenial setting when she ran away from Edmund.

She opened her eyes and closed the old register and put it back in the drawer on the teacher's desk until she could return it to Fred. She'd had to turn it in to the school board at the end of the school year, but had borrowed it back so she could be consistent this year with how she recorded everything. She admired consistency and tried to pass that value on to her students.

She had just finished her first day's lesson plans for the first three grades when she heard a horse approaching outside. Her heart skipped a beat. No reason to think it was Silas, but she always did. In spite of her best efforts to discourage him last year, he had insisted on courting her. Of course, she wasn't free to be courted but couldn't explain that to him. Even after Edmund appeared in the valley and tried to kill her, Silas refused to give up his pursuit of her. She had seen him a few times this summer in town, usually at the grocery when he came for supplies. He said Old Man Rickerts was poorly, so he couldn't get away from their place very often or for very long. Last year, Mr. Rickerts had sold his property to Silas for $1.50 in exchange for Silas's taking care of him until he died. She knew the bond between the two was very strong and that Silas would have taken care of him even without an incentive. The old man's body was failing rapidly.

Minta remembered Silas's words as he stood at the grocery counter talking about Rickerts. "His mind's still as sharp as ever, and he's still as ornery as ever," Silas said, "but his old body is just giving out. He tries to go out to do chores and, twice, I found him out in the corral fallen and not able to get up. The last time, I asked him what happened and he said, 'Death's pale rider done tried to throw a rope on me.'"

"I'm sorry, Silas," Minta said. She could imagine how hard it must be for Silas to see his mentor failing in health. "I know it's hard on you. And you'll miss him when he's gone."

"That's for sure. Can't imagine that place without him."

"Well, it's yours now, and I'm sure you'll make a fine ranch out of it."

"Sure would be nice if I had a woman to . . ."

"Silas, don't," Minta warned. "We've been over and over this. I'm not free to marry as long as Edmund's fate is up in the air, and you know I won't settle for anything less."

"I know," Silas said. "I just said it would be nice. It's a lonely place out there, even with Rickerts to talk to."

Lonely, Minta thought. Sometimes the schoolhouse was a lonely place, too, even with all the students to talk to. It was lonely and a little scary to be the only adult days on end.

Minta forced her mind back to the present, stood, and looked out the school window. After thinking of Silas so vividly, she expected to see him; instead she saw Mary, behind Angus, on their horse. Mary gave him the basket she was holding while she jumped down. Then he handed it down to her and dismounted himself. They were both a little taller than last year, and Mary had lost some of her baby fat. Their summer-bleached hair was almost white in the sun. All the Haley children had blond hair and blue eyes, but Angus and Mary were shorter than their cousins and stockier.

Minta went outside to greet them.

"Hi, Miss Mayfield," Mary said. "I'm so excited about school starting tomorrow. Here, Mother and Aunt Claudia sent you some food." She thrust out the basket. Minta took it and peeked inside— eggs and fresh butter along with a loaf of Claudia's bread. Angus and Mary's mother, Rachel, took care of the hen house and eggs, while Claudia did most of the baking.

"Thank you, Mary. And how about you, Angus, are you just as excited about school starting?" Minta asked with a twinkle in her eye.

He shot her a look that showed he caught her humor. "Oh, yeah," he said dryly, "haven't been able to sleep for weeks."

Mary giggled. A serious little girl, she seldom participated in the other kids' joking but appreciated it when she heard it. She surprised Minta by saying, "Well, good thing school's starting. You can catch up on your sleep in class."

"Are you kidding? That ol' teacher just keeps waking me up," Angus said.

Minta laughed. "Enough, Angus. You'll do fine this year. We've got to get you ready for the Eighth Grade Exams."

"Boy, am I dreading that! Can't I stay in seventh grade a couple more years?"

"You could. And if you don't apply yourself, you may. But don't you want to graduate and go on to high school?"

"I want to graduate, but I'm not sure about high school. All Honor talked about this summer is all the work she's going to have to do in high school this year." Honor, Fred and Claudia's oldest daughter, had been Minta's helper last year. Now she was off to Durango to high school, living with the Woods' family, taking care of the kids and helping with the housework in exchange for room and board.

"You know how Honor likes to exaggerate, Angus," Minta said. "But it will be difficult for her, having to keep house for the Woods' family in addition to her studies."

"Not much different than she did here," Mary said. "We all do a lot of work besides school."

"I know you do, dear. And it makes you better people."

"You sound just like Uncle Fred. It's good for our character, right?" Angus asked.

"That's right. You've all got a lot of character and more coming this year. Tell your mother and aunt Claudia 'thank you' for me. I can't wait to bite into this fresh bread. It smells so good! But tell them they don't have to be as generous as they were last year. I worked in the grocery all summer and saved up, as well as bringing a lot of supplies with me. I do appreciate the fresh eggs and milk and butter, though. This year I'll probably be going into Liberty most weekends, so I'll be able to replenish my goods. Which reminds me, I need to talk to your Uncle Fred about buying a horse. I want to go the shorter back trail to Liberty but don't want to walk."

"We're also supposed to ask you to come to supper tonight," Mary said. "You can ask him then. Six o'clock."

"Thank you. I'll see you again at six, then," Minta said. She was anxious to talk to Claudia and exchange news of their summers. It was so nice to have friends, a luxury Edmund had not allowed her. Minta was troubled that she wouldn't be able to tell Claudia about Lulabelle, though. She'd promised not to tell Lulabelle's secret to anyone, but Claudia was so wise about the ways of the world. She could help Lulabelle if she were given the chance.

Before returning to the schoolroom, Minta stood on the step and looked across to where the teacherage had stood. It still hurt to look at the black scar that had been her home last year. The school board men, Fred Haley, Jens Fredrickson, and Paulo Valori, who had taken Luke Wood's place, had cleaned up all the debris, but the earth was still blackened except where rain water had washed several deep scars across it. The opening to the dugout was more visible now. At least it had survived, so she had a cool place to store foodstuffs.

She turned and looked at the school building. A fresh coat of paint brightened the sides, and the roof was fixed where the fire had damaged it. Her shoulder brushed the bell rope. That was new this year, too. When the men added the room onto the school, they put a real bell up on a post by the front door. She was to ring it every morning at eight so the students knew they had fifteen minutes to get to school. The bell could be heard all over the valley on a calm day. Minta had been surprised at the bell, given the impoverished state of the school district. "Are you sure we can afford this?" she'd asked Fred when he showed her how to ring the bell most effectively as he was helping her move into her new room.

"We decided we couldn't afford *not* to have a bell," Fred said. "And you'll notice you didn't get the new readers you asked for. You'll have to make do with the old ones. We decided, after what happened last year when the teacherage burned, that we needed a way to summon the community in an emergency. You never know when a kid might fall in the creek or break a leg or something. That's why we don't want you to ring it except at eight a.m. Any other time we hear it, the whole community will come running."

Minta was humbled. She couldn't even complain about the readers. In spite of what he said, she knew they did it for her—for her safety. They knew she was still worried that Edmund might return, and they wanted to make her feel safe. It was comforting to know all she had to do was pull on a rope and people would come to her aid. Of course, that would mean she'd have to be able to get to the rope and then pull it.

After supper that evening Minta and Claudia headed for the twin rockers on the Haleys' porch to talk while the girls did the dishes. They could hear Mary bossing Judy in friendly tones. Rachel had gone back to her own cabin with a headache. Most days the two Haley households took their main meal together. It made less work for the two women. Rachel still hadn't recovered from her husband Richard's death, but was slowly reentering the close-knit world of the Rockytop community. She wasn't comfortable sitting and visiting like Claudia and Minta did, though, preferring to read or knit quietly on her own. Her two children, Angus and Mary, spent almost as much time at Fred and Claudia's as their own children did.

"I heard your cousin is with child, Minta," Claudia said when they were settled.

"Yes. Her baby's due just a month or so after yours, I think."

Claudia patted her growing stomach. "That can't come soon enough for me. This was a long, hot summer. Not the best time to be in this condition, let me tell you. How's your cousin doing? Isn't this her first?"

"Her name's Lulabelle," Minta said. "Yes, it's her first. I guess she's doing okay. She's a little . . . nervous."

"That's to be expected. Did you tell her what I told you last year? About fear of childbirth?"

"Yes. It's not the birth she fears so much as what might come after."

"Now, that's a smart woman. She's right to be fearful. Birthing is the easy part. It's the next eighteen years or so that's hard. Raising a child up right is a big job."

"Speaking of eighteen years. How's Richard doing? I noticed he wasn't here tonight." The Haley's oldest son, Richard, was only two years younger than Minta, but she felt much closer in age to his mother than to him.

"No, he's off seeing Sally Mae. I expect we'll be having us a wedding soon." She laughed. "I was up visiting Rickerts the other day—took him some of my cinnamon rolls he's so partial to. I guess Richard's been spending a lot of time talking to Silas. Rickerts said to me, 'That boy of yourn is plumb loco over a filly what's like to break him to double harness and hitch him to a plow'."

"Sally Mae? Wasn't she in Shady Rest School last year? I remember a Sally Mae from the softball game."

"That's her. He's been courting her all summer. Can't hardly get him to stay home long enough to get his clothes washed."

"But isn't she kind of young?"

"I think she's sixteen. I can't say much. I was sixteen when Richard was born. Sally Mae took several extra years to get through school. She finally finished eighth grade last year."

"Not as smart as your Honor, then." Minta said. "I'm so glad she gets to go to high school this year."

"Me, too," Claudia said, "but I wish she didn't have to go all the way to Durango. Heard Liberty might be getting a high school one of these days. Then she could at least come home weekends. We really miss her around here. Mary's a pretty good help but not like Honor was. I think she'll do fine taking care of the Woods' kids."

"I think so, too. And she'll make a fine teacher when she gets out of school. She was a big help to me last year. Well, I suppose I ought to head on down the road before it gets dark. Thank you for the supper."

Minta stood, but Claudia stayed put and asked, "Have you seen Silas since you got back?"

"No. I don't expect to, either. You know there's nothing between us."

"There's a lot between you, Minta. You just won't admit it. Silas is a good man. He could . . ."

"Silas could be the King of England for all the good it would do me. You know I can't look at another man—and why."

"I know, Minta. I'm sorry."

"Not half as sorry as I am. Is Fred in the barn? I want to talk to him about a horse. Then I'll head on home."

Loud giggles came through the open door along with sounds of splashing.

"I guess I'd better go referee those girls," Claudia said as she stood and turned to go back into the kitchen. "Judy, if you break that plate,

I'll break your you-know-what," she called as she disappeared through the door.

Minta found Fred and asked about buying a horse.

"I've got one I could loan you on weekends, Minta. Where would you keep a horse down there?"

"I thought I could keep it down by the creek like the kids do when they ride to school."

"That's fine for now, but what about this winter? You'd need a barn, and feed for it."

"I hadn't thought of that. But letting me take one every weekend, that's awfully generous of you. What could I do in return?"

"Just what you always do—teach the kids."

"I get paid for that. I mean, for you, in exchange for using the horse."

"I don't know. I'll think of something. I'll have the kids bring Molly to school on Fridays. Then you can ride into town after school Friday or on Saturday morning. Drop her off on Sunday on your way back. She's too old to be much good working the place, but she's still rideable. She was mostly Honor's horse anyway, and now she's away she don't get rode often enough. You'll be doing us a favor."

"Oh, Fred, I know better than that. But I do thank you, and I'll find some way to repay you if you don't think of something first."

"You know we don't keep track around here. Just help when you can, and we'll do the same."

"I know. That's why I love it here." Minta smiled all the way home.

CHAPTER FOUR

If Wishes Were Horses

Wednesday, September 15, 1920, Rockytop—*Oh, diary, I'm sorry it's been so long since I've written. I feel as if I haven't stopped running since school started. I reread my last few entries and was embarrassed I had said how much easier this school year would be. I couldn't have been more wrong. The Stonacre children are a handful, and I haven't even met the oldest, Solly, yet. Apparently they aren't going to allow him to start school until October because of the fall work on their place. He's already far behind where he should be in school. I haven't met the parents, either. They didn't come to the back-to-school potluck we had. Fred said they probably had too much to do getting the Archuleta place fixed up the way they want it. I know, I need to quit calling it the Archuleta place. It's the Stonacres' now. How I wish I had my little Archuleta girls back, though.*

"If wishes were horses, beggars would ride," Grandmother used to say, "so quit wishing and get to work."

Minta rang the eight o'clock bell, carried the two water buckets inside, one for drinking and one for washing, and started writing the day's lessons on the blackboard. When it was time to ring the small handbell to call the children inside, they were all there except Angus and Michael, who were up in the mountains helping with the fall gathering of cattle, and the Stonacres, who were often late. It seemed Clara tried to get the younger ones there on time but was often unsuccessful. The other children were just sitting down after the morning exercises—

pledging the flag and singing two patriotic hymns—when the Stonacres walked in.

"Clara, I'd like to speak with you privately at recess," Minta said.

"Yes'm," Clara mumbled into her chest.

"You better not hit my sister," Everett said. He and Clara were the most verbal of the Stonacres. It was hard to get any of the rest of them to say more than "yes'm" and "no'm."

"I'm not going to hit Clara, Everett," Minta said. "I just wish to talk with her. Now all of you get out your readers and begin your lessons."

The morning passed quickly as Minta went from one group to another, helping, answering questions, and scolding those who needed to get back to the work they were supposed to be doing. It was a relief to send them out for first recess.

Clara stayed sitting in her desk, looking down at her roughened hands as she twisted a piece of paper back and forth. Minta wondered if Clara was as aware of the dirty fingernails as she was. The girl's unwashed, mouse-brown hair hung down over her eyes, as usual, and Minta had to keep herself from pushing it back. Clara was an awkward girl who didn't have good posture and seldom made eye contact. There were so many things Minta would like to work on with her but, first, she had to win her trust.

"Clara, dear," Minta said. She tried not to use her teacher voice. "Do you think you could get yourselves here on time more often?"

"We try, ma'am. Sometimes there's just too much to do before we can git gone. Like today the pigs got out and we had to go chasing them all over."

"Okay, I understand that those things can happen. But do try to be more prompt, all right?"

"Yes'm. Can I go now?"

"*May* you go now. Not yet. I'm wondering when might be a good time for me to come visit your folks? I'd like to talk to them about Solly starting school sooner, or at least having some of his lessons sent home so that he doesn't get so far behind. I could send them home with you. Since you're in the same grade, you could explain the lessons to him if he doesn't understand."

"I could take them home, but he wouldn't do them. He don't do nothing but what somebody makes him."

"That's why I'd like to talk to your parents, Clara. Perhaps if I told them how important it . . ."

"That's not a good idea. Pa don't like people coming over," Clara said.

"Then maybe I could just visit with your mother, and . . ."

Clara looked up in alarm. "Oh, no! That's an even worse idea. It's best if you just do what you can with us here at school. I know we ain't very good students, but I'd like to keep coming ifin we can. It's nice here."

"I wasn't suggesting you not come to school, Clara."

Minta let Clara go out with the others and sat at her desk thinking. It wouldn't do to let the situation continue. She'd have to go talk to the parents. Should she ask Fred, as the president of the school board, to go with her? No. That might look like she was trying to gang up on them. She would go alone, try to be firm but friendly, make her case, and see what happened—maybe after school tomorrow.

Minta still hadn't decided whether to go or not the next day when the Stonacre children were even later than usual. She'd about decided her conversation with Clara had scared them away for good when they came in, sliding into their seats as quietly as possible, while the second and third graders were reading aloud to Minta.

"Everett and Dennis, get your reading books open to page thirty-two and come join us," Minta said.

Everyone waited while Everett rummaged in the cubbyhole under the top of his desk.

"What's the matter, Everett?" Minta asked.

"Can't find no book," Everett said, his head almost entirely inside the opening.

Minta got up and walked over to him. She reached down and took hold of his shoulder to get his head out of the desk so she could look.

"Ow!" he hollered, banging his head on the desk as he jerked back away from her. "Don't you touch me!" He cringed away from her in the desk, holding his shoulder as if she'd burned him by touching him.

"Don't hurt him, Teacher," Clara said, jumping up out of her seat. "I'll find the dumb book."

"Sit down, Clara! The book can wait. Everett, come back to the cloakroom with me. I'd like to talk with you. And, yes, I just want to talk. No, Clara, I said sit down."

"Please let me come, too," Clara said. Something about the way she said it convinced Minta it would be a good idea.

"All right, Clara, you may come, too. Mary, will you listen to the primaries read? They're on page thirty-two. The rest of you continue with your lessons."

In the cloakroom, Minta sat Everett in the chair she kept there for when she needed to remove someone from the classroom. She and Clara stood on each side of him.

"Now, Everett, what was that all about?" Minta asked.

"You hurt me," he said, still holding his shoulder with one hand.

"I couldn't possibly have hurt you," Minta said. "I merely touched you, so you'd know I was there and could get out of my way."

"Did, too," Everett said stubbornly. "My shoulder really, really hurts. You probably done scarred me up."

"Everett!" Clara and Minta said together.

"Everett, don't," Clara said. "Sorry, ma'am. He doesn't know what he's saying."

"Do too," Everett said. "She's a mean teacher that likes to hit kids. I heard the big boys talking about what she done last year."

"The big boys exaggerate," Minta said. "All I did was go like this." She reached out to touch his shoulder again.

"No!" Everett cried, cringing away from her. As he did, Minta noticed a faint trace of blood on his shirt.

"Don't touch him, ma'am," Clara said. "Really it would be better if . . ."

"Take off your shirt, Everett," Minta said. "I want to see something."

"No!" both Stonacre children cried at once.

A cold dread filled Minta. She was pretty sure what she'd find, but she had to see for herself. "Take off your shirt, Everett. Now!"

He looked at her defiantly, but when she didn't back down, he slowly undid the three buttons that remained on the ragged shirt and slipped it off.

Minta looked down on the fresh welts on top of old scars, tears in her eyes. She knew, because of Edmund, what caused wounds like that—probably a cane or stick of some kind.

"Is this why you were late today?" Minta asked Clara.

"Yes'm," Clara said, hanging her head.

"It was my fault," Everett said. "I didn't get my chores done fast enough."

"Did your father do this to you, or your mother?"

"It doesn't matter," Clara said. "I'll help Everett with his chores tomorrow, and maybe we won't be so late."

"I asked you a question. Who did this?"

Both kids looked at the floor and refused to answer.

"I'm going to walk home with you today after school. I'd like to speak to your parents about . . ."

"No!" Clara said. "You'll just make everything worse. Don't talk to them!"

"I was going to say 'speak to them about Solly starting school'; I won't say anything to upset them, I promise." If anyone knew how to talk to abusive people, it was Minta. She had survived over a year of

Edmund's abuse by learning what was safe to say and do. She could use those skills with the Stonacres—she hoped.

The problems she'd been having with the Stonacre children were now put into perspective. Their shyness, the way they stuck together and avoided the other kids at recess, the way they always moved away from her when she approached them could all be attributed to how they were treated at home. At first Minta had thought they acted that way because they were new in school, but the newness should have worn off by now. They should be opening up, making friends. Clara's words came back to Minta: "I'd like to keep coming. It's nice here." She'd have to be careful not to say anything that would cause the Stonacres to pull their children out of school.

After school, Clara and Minta walked together while the rest of the Stonacre children trailed along behind them. Everett complained and kicked clods of dirt all the way up the hill toward Piñon Hollow. "You're going to get me in more trouble, Teacher," he said. Minta tried to reassure him, but it did no good. It took a good half-hour to walk, and they were all tired and panting by the time they reached the buildings.

When they neared the house, Minta asked, "Where would I find your parents this time of day?"

"Ma will be in the house, probably the kitchen," Clara answered. "Pa could be anywhere. You kids run in and change to your work clothes, and git after your chores," she ordered her siblings. Minta wondered what clothes they had that were rougher than the ones they wore to school. She thought they came in their work clothes.

As the kids ran into the house, Minta and Clara entered the kitchen. "Ma!" Clara yelled. "Ma, someone's here."

A small, bent woman with a dirty scarf tied around hair as limp and dull as Clara's came into the kitchen. From what Minta knew from her time at the Archuletas', the room she came out of was the back bedroom. A yellowish bruise covered one cheekbone, and her hands shook as she stood looking at Minta with dismay. A little boy of three or four clung to her skirt with one hand. She held a baby balanced on one hip.

"Ma, this here's the teacher. I tried to talk her outa coming," Clara said by way of introduction.

"Pleased to meet you." Minta stuck out her hand which was ignored. "Please, call me Minta, Mrs. Stonacre." The woman didn't offer her first name. "I'm sorry to intrude, but since you didn't come to the potluck, I wanted to meet you and tell you how happy I am to have your children in school this year." She waited to be offered a chair. A drink after the long, dusty walk would be nice, too. She was offered neither.

"You can't be here," the woman finally said in a raspy voice. "We got work to do. Clara, there's taters waiting on the back porch to be peeled. Take these young'uns with you."

"Yes'm," Clara said, taking her brother's hand and balancing the baby on her hip in an imitation of her mother. They disappeared through the doorway, leaving Minta to her own devices.

"I'll only take a few minutes of your time, Mrs. Stonacre. I wanted to talk to you about Solly. I'd like to help him catch up on his studies if he's going to miss all of September."

The kitchen door banged open, and the room darkened as the opening filled with the bulk of Sol, Senior. Minta turned and looked up at the man she'd seen on the street in Liberty. In the confines of the small kitchen, he looked taller and bulkier than she remembered. Before she could offer a pleasant greeting, he said, "You got business here, lady, you take it up with me. Don't be bothering my wife; she's got work to do." As if on cue, the woman turned abruptly and exited the kitchen through the same door Clara had used.

Minta wanted to say, "And you don't?" but held her tongue. She turned back to Sol and looked up and into eyes she would recognize anywhere. The cold, hard eyes of a man like Edmund. Instead she said,

"As you've probably surmised, I'm the Rockytop teacher and I'm here about Solly. I think it would . . ."

"You using big words to impress me, lady? I 'surmise' it would be a good idea for you to take yourself back where you came from. Good day." He turned his back to her and started back out the kitchen door. Surprisingly, Minta realized she wasn't afraid of this man. He didn't have the power over her that Edmund had. While the law would look the other way at a man mistreating his own wife or children, it wouldn't look the other way if he mistreated her, the teacher. And he knew it, too. No, she wasn't afraid of him.

"Mr. Stonacre, I'm sorry if we've gotten off on the wrong foot. I'd just like to do what's best for your children. And I'd like your help. It's obvious that you're a well-educated man. I'm sure you'd like your children to be, also."

He stopped and turned back around. "Yeah, I would. That's *your* job. You can do whatever you want with them when they're in your school. The rest of the time, you leave them, and my wife, alone. You got that?"

She opened her mouth to reply, but he was already striding across the yard toward the barn, and she knew he wouldn't answer her. "That went well," she said aloud, but no one answered her sarcasm. Clara and Mrs. Stonacre had disappeared, and the house had that quiet, empty feeling. She knew where the well was, and she went outside to draw herself a drink to fortify her for the long walk back to Rockytop. She had accomplished little more than meeting the Stonacres. But she couldn't get the image of Mrs. Stonacre out of her mind. If she'd had children by Edmund, if she hadn't escaped Edmund . . . *There, but for the grace of God, go I,* she thought.

CHAPTER FIVE

A Burden Shared

❧

Sunday, September 26, 1920, Liberty—*I realized I hardly think of Edmund any more during the week at school; I'm too busy. On weekends, however, when I visit Lulabelle and see her struggling with regaining her speech and with her pregnancy, I can't help but think of him. Each week that goes by with no news increases the likelihood that he is dead. I know Sheriff Upton is getting tired of my asking for news since, to him, the case is closed. I wish I could be as sure as he is.*

Lulabelle is improving even though she doesn't see it. Since I only see her once a week, or less, I can see the differences. Her speech is getting less hesitant, and she doesn't tire as easily. She's just frustrated by not being able to do all she did before. I help her all I can, but so much of her recovery will require time and patience, something Lulabelle's not noted for. She's a little more hopeful about the upcoming birth, however, since I explained it's unlikely Edmund is the father. I'm sure once she holds the little one in her arms, all will be well.

I'm still staying at Matthew and Miriam's when I'm in town. Frank and Lulabelle's place is too small. I appreciate the Posts' hospitality and the chance to seek their counsel. As Superintendent of Schools, Matthew is very aware of the problems teachers face.

Minta had been waiting to hear Matthew come in. She put down her pen when she heard the door shut downstairs and rose to go speak with him.

"Hello, Minta," he greeted her. "Is Miriam not back yet?"

"No. She said she might be a while as she was going to stop by the hotel to visit with Mrs. Whiteside on the way back. You know how hard it is to get away from that woman!"

Matthew chuckled. "Indeed I do. Miriam's a dear to continue to visit her."

"I'll fix us some tea," Minta said. "There's something I'd like to discuss with you."

When they were seated at the kitchen table sipping their tea, Minta told Matthew about her visit with the Stonacres and about the children's problems in school.

"That's a hard one," Matthew said. "We can't really interfere with a man's discipline of his children, even if we feel it's excessive."

"His wife had bruises, too," Minta reminded him.

"But we don't really know what caused them. We weren't there. We can suspect, but that's all. Unless he causes enough injury to get a doctor involved . . ."

"It's so unfair!" Minta protested.

"I know it is, but my hands are tied. And I think you need to be very careful about what you do and say—to the children as well as to their parents."

"Isn't there *anything* I can do?"

"Just love the kids when they're under your care. Show them that the whole world isn't against them. And if they do come to school with serious injuries, we might be able to get Doc and Mo to do something. I read in the paper the other day about a man who beat up his wife down at the train station in Durango. They arrested him."

"They did? What happened then?"

"He got fined—twenty-two dollars."

"Twenty-two dollars? For beating up his wife?"

"Well, at least it's something, Minta. May make him think twice next time. May make people like Stonacre think twice, too."

"I doubt Sol Stonacre reads the Durango paper. And if he seriously injured any of the children, I doubt he'd send them to school where I'd see them. He'd keep them home."

"You're probably right. I know it sounds uncaring, Minta, but all you can do is your job. You have a whole school of students. You have to give your best to each of them. You can't save them from the cruelty of the world. But you can teach them to be strong, competent people who can deal with the world on its terms."

"Thank you, Matthew. I always feel better after talking to you."

"I wish all the teachers under my supervision were as caring and skilled as you are, Minta. You found the right calling when you decided to become a teacher."

"Thank you, but I didn't decide. I was forced into it."

"No, you decided. You could have run off and become a lady of the night instead of a teacher."

"Matthew!" Minta could feel the warmth as her cheeks turned red.

"Just kidding, Minta. But your reaction says it all. You became what you were called to. You couldn't have done anything else."

Minta returned to Rockytop feeling as if part of the burden had been lifted by sharing it with Matthew. She enjoyed the horseback ride along the back trail through the piñon and juniper forest. There were two small creeks to ford and beautiful views of the gray-green mesas off toward New Mexico as she rode south. Soon, however, the weather would be such that she'd have to decide if she really wanted to go so far on horseback. She seldom met anyone; most people took the longer route past Shady Rest School and back up Halpern Creek because the road was better or to pick up their mail.

The Rockytop area residents had set a pole at what was now called Tin Can Corner, and each attached a lard bucket for their mail. The Rural Free Delivery driver drove up from Halpern to the corner, which was as far as the road was regularly passable, and delivered the mail. Then whoever went by would pick up everyone else's and deliver it on the way home—except for Stonacres'. Sol had made it clear he didn't want anyone else picking up his mail. So what little he got sat there until he went by.

The Haleys usually brought Minta her mail. Her mother in Indiana wrote to her regularly now that Minta was no longer trying to conceal her whereabouts from Edmund. Frank had tried to get her parents to move to Liberty with him and Lulabelle. As much as they wanted to be nearer Minta and Lulabelle, they just couldn't bring themselves to leave their home of forty years. They were planning a trip to Liberty, though, to coincide with the birth of Lulabelle's child. They were surrogate parents to Lulabelle since her parents had both died before she reached adulthood. Minta was looking forward to seeing her parents and to her mother's help in the event things did not go well with the birth, or afterward.

The last downhill stretch into the Halpern Valley took Minta to the Haleys' property. Mary was picking wildflowers along the road, and Minta stopped the horse to get down to greet the girl.

"Those are pretty," Minta said.

"I'm going to take them to Mother. She likes flowers. They cheer her up, and she needs a lot of cheering up."

"I'm sure having such a sweet daughter cheers her up, too," Minta said.

Mary smiled shyly. Like most of the children, she wasn't used to compliments.

"Mary," Minta said, "I'd like you to try harder to make friends with Clara."

"I did try when school first started. She just wants to be off by herself at recess."

"I don't think she *wants* to, Mary. I think she doesn't know how to make friends. You could show her."

"How?"

"Well, find something she's interested in and be interested in it, too."

"Like what? When she won't even talk to me, how do I figure out what she's interested in?"

Minta visualized the classroom and the students' interactions with her and each other. "The only thing I can think of," she said, "is that Clara seems to like when we sing the songs each morning. Once I walked over and stood by her, and she has a sweet voice, even though she doesn't sing very loudly. Maybe she's interested in music."

"I was wanting to ask if you'd give me piano lessons like you did Honor last year," Mary said. "Maybe you could give us music lessons together. I could get permission to stay after school one day a week."

"I don't think Clara could stay after," Minta said. "Maybe I could give you lessons sometimes at recess. Would you be willing to give up recess a couple times a week?"

"Sure," Mary said, "and I'll bet if I tell Clara the teacher said she's a good singer, she would, too. We could learn to read music like Honor did."

Mary didn't waste any time. The very next day she approached Clara with the music lesson idea. To Minta's surprise, Clara agreed to try it at afternoon recess. She said she wasn't interested in learning to play the piano, but she did want to learn to read music and to sing better. The way she put it was, "I probably won't never have me a piany, but I'll always have my voice. I can sing anywhere."

Now Minta's problem was how to supervise the other children while she was busy with Clara and Mary. She'd gotten into the habit of letting the older girls watch over the younger ones. Well, childcare didn't have to be a job just for females. She asked Angus and Michael to stay a minute before they went out to recess.

"I'm putting you two boys in charge of recess this afternoon. If you do a good job, I'll let you continue organizing the afternoon recesses. I want you to set up some games everyone can play and make sure everyone participates. Well, maybe not Gina and Beth—they can play off in the little kids' corner by themselves if they'd rather, as long as you keep an eye on them."

"Okay, sure," Michael said, "we're needing to get everyone back to practicing softball anyway. We've *got* to beat Halpern this year."

"That's okay part of the time, but I want you to do other games and activities sometimes for those who don't always want to play softball."

"Who wouldn't want to play softball?" Angus asked.

"You'd be surprised, Angus," Minta said. "Softball is not the most important thing in the world to everyone. Just make it fun for them, and they'll do what you want."

Minta went outside and told the rest of the students that Michael and Angus were in charge and that she expected everyone to cooperate with them. When she went back inside, Mary and Clara had their heads bent over a piece of sheet music trying to figure out what all the symbols meant, so Minta started with having them copy the symbols on the board. Then she explained sharps, flats and all the rest to them and had them make a copy of everything on their own paper to keep in their desks to study. By then recess was over.

After school she asked Angus how things had gone.

"Okay, I guess. Well, at first the Stonacres didn't want to do what the rest of us were doing, but then me and Michael started playing catch with the softball. When I caught Everett looking our way, I threw it to him and told him to throw it to Dennis. Pretty soon we were all playing Running the Bases Tag. You remember that game we invented last year where the bases are safe and you have to run from one to the other without getting tagged?"

"I remember," Minta smiled. "That was when our ball was lost. Before Silas brought the new one."

"Yeah, you made us that rag ball, remember? That was the awfulest ball I ever tried to play with. I was real mad about our ball being gone. That's why I got in trouble."

"I know, Angus. But you got over it. So you all played tag today? Even the girls?"

"Eleanor didn't want to play. You know she usually just follows Clara around at recess. She went over and messed around with Gina and Beth for awhile. They were playing house like they always do. Finally, I guess Eleanor got bored, 'cause pretty soon she was playing with us, too. I told her she ran pretty good, for a girl. Might make a ball player out of her."

"Thank you, Angus. You boys did a good job. I'll be relying on you to help out at recess more often."

"Yes, ma'am. I don't mind. It's a chance to boss them around without them telling me I'm being bossy, since you said I could."

All in all, Minta felt good about the way the day had gone. She was just sorry she had to send the Stonacre children home at the end of it.

Chapter Six

Gossiping Girls

ᴄᴡᵃᴡᴩ

Tuesday, October 5, 1920, Rockytop—*Solly's first day of school yesterday was a disaster. He was determined to test me every chance he got. He's as tall as I am and outweighs me by quite a bit. He looks and acts so much like his father I find it hard to treat him as any other student. I fear I overestimated when I put him in seventh grade. He's much behind Michael and even Clara, and that is part of the problem. Whenever it was time for him to participate in class, he misbehaved to avoid having to show the other kids how little he knows. I know he's physically stronger than I am, and don't think beating him would do much good anyway. I'm sure my poor efforts with the ferule would be of little consequence to him compared to his father's beatings. I'll have to find another way to convince him to obey.*

Today I will ask Angus and Michael to try to befriend him as the other children have started to do with his siblings. It's been a joy watching them come out of their shells and start interacting with the other students both at recess and in the classroom. I am placing much hope in the power of softball to win Solly over to school and to my teaching. If he's not interested in softball, I don't know what I will do with him. I know Fred always says I can call him in if I need help with an unruly student, but I don't want to do that.

On a happier note, I have finally decided on the Christmas program. It's past time we got started on it. I know people will expect something good after the success of last year's play. I despaired of having a play this year because I fear all the Stonacres will have the same problem with stage fright that Angus did last year. One recess I noticed Angus carving one of the wooden figures he's so good at and some of the girls sewing doll clothes out of scraps of material. That gave me the idea to do a puppet show. The children will make the puppets, I'll write the script, and they'll provide the voices, but behind a screen, so they won't see the audience looking at them.

After morning exercises Minta announced to the students her plans for the Christmas program. "We will start working on it every Friday beginning this week," she said.

"Do we all have to do puppets?" Clara asked.

"Well, some of you might have other things to do in the program. For example, Clara, I had hoped you would sing a song, but you can do both."

"I don't want to sew any puppet costumes," Clara said.

"Why not?"

"At our house we all have our work. I'm the cooker. Eleanor's the sewer. She's real good at it, too."

"I'm glad to know that. We'll all rely on Eleanor's skills in making the costumes. She can teach those of us who aren't expert seamstresses."

Eleanor looked down at her desk, her face flushed, but she couldn't hide her smile.

"Do all the boys get to carve the heads?" Dale asked. Minta was still getting used to the new, more grown-up Dale. He'd lost most of the baby-talk over the summer and learned to pronounce his "r's."

"All the boys who are allowed to carry knives to school may do so. If your parents don't allow you to carry a knife yet, you aren't old enough to use it safely. But there will be lots of other ways you'll be able to help." Dale kicked the leg of his chair in disappointment.

"I'm not carving no puppet," Solly said.

"Probably his mommy doesn't let him carry a knife, yet," Michael said to Angus just loudly enough for most of the class to hear.

"Michael," Minta said in her sternest voice, "that will do." She turned to write Michael's name on the board—his first strike for the day in her Three Strikes and You're Out punishment plan.

While her back was turned, Solly stood up, reached deep into his pocket, and pulled out a knife. He flipped open the blade and thrust it toward Michael, "Want to see my knife, Mikey?"

"Solly, don't," Clara said.

Eleanor started to cry. "You're going to get us kicked out of this school, too, Solly," she sobbed, "and I don't want to go. I *like* it here!"

"No one is getting kicked out, *yet*," Minta said. "Solly, I'm glad to see you have a knife and will be able to help with the puppets after all. But we won't be starting until Friday, so put it away for now."

"I said I ain't doing no dumb puppets," Solly said, as he put the knife back in his pocket.

"I guess he don't know how to carve," Michael said. "Maybe he could help Dale and the other little kids with whatever you're going to have them do."

Minta glared at Michael and put an X by his name while Solly shouted, "I do, too! I carved an eagle just the other day, didn't I Clara?"

"Yeah. It even looks like a bird," Clara said.

"That's settled then," Minta said. "We'd love to see your eagle, Solly. Could you bring it to school tomorrow? Now, everyone, get out your books. The assignments are on the board. Solly, I want to start with you reading to me in the cloakroom so we don't disturb the others. Clara and Angus are in charge while I'm gone. I'm sure none of you wants your name to join Michael's on the board, so get busy."

Minta listened as Solly stumbled his way through a story that Minta knew was written at the fourth grade level. "That's fine, Solly," she said when he was done. "You know most of the words. You just need more practice. Maybe you could read to the little ones at home sometimes. How old are they and what are their names?"

"Charlie's four and Gracie's one," Solly mumbled. "Doubt they'd sit still to be read at."

"I'll bet they'd love to have your attention and would sit still for you. I'm sure they look up to you as do all your brothers and sisters here at school."

"Clara don't. She's too independent for her own good. Pa says."

"Well, she's growing up, as you are. You'll both be making your way in the world soon. A good education will help you do that. I really want you to do well here, Solly. It would be a shame to have to ask you to leave when you have so much you could offer the other kids."

"What do you mean? I don't offer them nothing."

"Your experience and your physical abilities. I'll bet you'd be really good at softball, for example. Have you ever played it?"

"Sure. At some of our other schools I did. 'Til we got kicked out or pulled out. It's just a dumb game."

"Maybe it just seemed that way to you because you didn't get to stay for the all-school tournament at the end of the year. I'll bet you could be a big factor in helping Rockytop beat Halpern this year. Those boys at Halpern like to make fun of Rockytop. They say we're a bunch of country bumpkins who can't throw or hit straight. Sure would be nice to prove them wrong." She hoped she had appealed to Solly's competitive nature. Time would tell.

At recess Minta walked around enjoying the fall sun. October was a beautiful month in Colorado with a number of hardy wildflowers which had survived the first frost blooming at the bases of the yellow cottonwoods and willows along the creek. The aspens on the La Plata Mountains in the distance covered the slopes with gold. She still hadn't been able to make a trip up into the mountains. Maybe this weekend she and Lulabelle could talk Frank into taking them up for a picnic.

Most of the boys were playing softball in the back field, and Minta listened to the crack of bat hitting ball as she walked. Even Solly was playing, although he and Michael were keeping a wary distance from each other. She could see problems developing between the two of them with Angus in the middle. Angus was making an attempt to befriend Solly as she'd asked, but that seemed to make Michael mad. He was used to having Angus all to himself.

Clara, Mary, Gertie, and Eleanor were giggling in the shade of the schoolhouse as Minta turned and walked back closer to the school.

"Does, too," Eleanor was saying. "We seen her with our own eyes, didn't we, Clara?"

"Yep," Clara said. "She was hanging out the wash—his *underwear!*" Another round of giggles followed the pronouncement of that word.

"You're lying," Mary said indignantly. "Silas doesn't have a wife."

Minta stopped in her tracks, knowing she should quit listening, but drawn in by wanting to know what they were discussing.

"Didn't say she was his wife," Clara said, "but he's got a woman living there. She's there first thing in the morning and last thing at night, and she washes his unmentionables; that's all I know. Who would do that 'cept a wife or a pretend one?"

"Have you met her?" Gertie asked.

"No. We can see their yard from our upper pasture. We see her from a distance when we're taking the cows out or bringing 'em back. One time we seen him ride up to her on his horse and bend down and kiss her!"

"Well, if Silas had gotten married, I'm sure we'd know about it," Mary said. "My cousin Richard's getting married next month and it's all anyone talks about. When could Silas have gotten married without us knowing?"

"Maybe that week he was gone," Gertie said. "A week before the cattle gathering he went somewheres. I know 'cause Ma went up and took care of Old Man Rickerts every day, and Pa and Ernst done the chores."

Minta gritted her teeth. She didn't know which made her madder: Gertie's bad grammar when she definitely knew better or the girls' gossiping. The Stonacres' grammar was having a bad influence on the other students, and Clara seemed to be a gossip. The fact that they were gossiping about Silas was even worse. The last thing Minta wanted to hear about was Silas and another woman.

"I'll bet that's it," Clara said. "He met this woman when he was gone and brung her back here. Maybe they got married; maybe they didn't. Some men and women live together what ain't married."

"That's enough!" Minta made her presence known to the girls. "You know better than to gossip about your neighbors."

Gertie turned to Eleanor who was fast becoming her friend and confidant. "Miss Mayfield's just mad 'cause she's sweet on Silas," she whispered, but Minta caught the main points.

"Gertie, what did I say? Do you want your name on the board?"

"No, ma'am," she said obediently. But Minta heard the giggles as the girls walked away. She didn't understand why their conversation had angered her so. Was Silas the one she was really mad at? She had told him he needed a woman to help with the ranch, so why, now, was she so disappointed to hear he'd taken her advice? Was it because of the suggestion he was living in sin, or was it that his vow to wait for her had lasted such a short time? Minta didn't want to face the answer. She turned back to the school—her hiding place. Last year she'd been hiding from Edmund. What was she hiding from now?

CHAPTER SEVEN

Silas's New Woman

Monday, October 18, 1920, Rockytop—*Our trip to the La Plata Mountains Sunday was wonderful. I haven't seen Lulabelle so happy and relaxed since she moved here. Her baby wasn't relaxed, though; it was kicking up a storm. She let Frank and me put our hands on her stomach and feel the kicks. I had no idea babies did that. Frank said he was kicking to get out so he could see the mountains, too. Frank seems convinced the baby will be a boy. I hope he's not too disappointed if that's not the case.*

I told Frank and Lulabelle I won't be able to continue to come to Liberty every weekend. For one thing, I've got to stay for Richard and Sally Mae's wedding, as I'm playing the piano for it. And there's so much to do to get ready for the Christmas program. I hope Lulabelle doesn't choose that day to have her baby, even though I'd like it to be early for her sake. I want to be with her for the birth, if possible, and I'd like for her and Frank to see Rockytop. They haven't been out here yet, as starting up a new business takes all their time. The best news is my parents will be here for the program and stay through the birth and the first few weeks when Lulabelle will need the most help. I'm so excited to see them.

School has settled into a routine. Most of the students are doing well. Solly still struggles academically but seems to be making some effort, at least. I think Angus is becoming a good influence on him. Solly and Michael almost came to blows the other day. I don't relish having to break up a fight between those two. I hope what I was told in Normal School is correct, that the best way to break up a fight between two big boys is to get in between them, since they won't hit a woman. Solly is still difficult, but he stops just short of doing something that will get him expelled. Dare I hope that he's joined his sisters in thinking school is a better place to be than home? He came in one day last week with bruises on his face and arms. When asked, he said he'd fallen off a horse. It reminded me of Edmund trying to explain the injuries he'd given me as being the result of a horse accident. I must figure out a way to approach the parents, so I can intervene on the children's behalf.

Minta closed her diary and opened her Bible. She still started every day with Bible reading and, if time, writing in her diary. The two books were her most important possessions and what had kept her sane at Edmund's. She smiled when she thought of how she'd hidden her diary from him behind a loose board in the outhouse.

She had been working her way through the New Testament since school started. She was up to Chapter Six in Ephesians. Verse four read: *And, ye fathers, provoke not your children to wrath: but bring them up in the nurture and admonition of the Lord.* Minta wondered if the Stonacres ever went to church. She hadn't seen them at the church in Halpern the few Sundays she hadn't been in Liberty. She missed that little Methodist Church and Reverend MacIntosch and would be glad to get back to going there more often. Since Claire Carpenter had moved and Minta wasn't usually there, the wife of Ben Griffith, Halpern School's teacher, had been playing piano for the services.

Minta pulled her thoughts back to her reading. Verses 13-17 seemed to be telling her what to do about the Stonacres:

> *Wherefore take unto you the whole armour of God, that ye may be able to withstand in the evil day, and having done all, to stand. And your feet shod with the preparation of the gospel of peace; Above all, taking the shield of faith, wherewith ye shall be able to quench all the fiery darts of the evil one. And take the helmet of salvation, and the sword of the Spirit, which is the word of God.*

Her grandmother always told her to "put on the armour of God." Last spring, when Edmund tracked her down and attempted to kill her,

God had led her to a place of safety. She was learning more and more to depend on God, to listen when He spoke to her through her Bible reading and prayer. The word of God would be her sword; and her faith, her shield. No, she wasn't afraid of the Stonacres. They needed to hear the gospel of peace. She bent her head in prayer.

After school each day last year, two children, one older and one younger, stayed a few minutes to help her clean the boards and floor. She hadn't started that routine yet this year because she was concerned it might cause trouble at home for the Stonacre children. If Sol was as much like Edmund as she suspected, the children would have to be home from school by a certain time each day or face their father's wrath. It wouldn't be fair to the other children to have them do the work and not the Stonacres, so Minta did it herself.

She was sweeping when she heard someone coming on horseback. No point running to the window—it wouldn't be Silas. He apparently had all the female companionship he needed at home. She kept sweeping determinedly until she heard the door open.

"Minta," she heard Fred call from the cloakroom, "could I talk to you a minute?" She had known it wouldn't be Silas. So why was she so disappointed to hear Fred's voice?

"Sure, Fred, come in," Minta replied. "Let's pull a couple chairs over by the windows."

Fred took off his hat and self-consciously rubbed his hand over his balding head. His hair must have once been as blond as the kids' but was now a weary gray. His work-worn hands settled the hat in his lap as he sat down.

When she was seated, Fred said, "I've been hearing you're having problems with the Stonacre kids."

"I haven't complained," Minta said.

"No, you haven't. But I know you. You're too stubborn to ask for help even if you need it."

"So, what have you heard? And from whom?" Minta asked.

"Well, Michael said that oldest boy is always causing trouble and even pulled a knife on him one day."

"Michael said that, did he? And did he also happen to mention what he said to make Solly so mad?"

"No. I guess I should have known there was more to it than just Michael's side. I'm sorry, Minta. Why don't you tell me what really happened?"

Minta told him the whole story of the Stonacres from their first days in school, to Solly's arrival, to her visit to their house, to her conversation with Matthew.

Fred frowned when she told him about Matthew. "Why didn't you come to me first, Minta," he asked, "instead of going over my head to Matthew?"

"I didn't think of it as going over your head. I was in town, staying at his house, and he's always so wise. I just thought he might have some good advice. I'm sorry if I offended you."

"Well, no harm done, I guess. But something's got to be done about that boy. We can't have him terrorizing you and the other kids. You know, just say the word and I'll come over and straighten him out."

"He's not terrorizing anyone. In fact, he's gotten much better with me, and . . . well . . . with everyone, except Michael. Those two just seem to rub each other the wrong way."

"You might have to let them settle it on their own—fight it out."

"No, Fred! I couldn't do that. I don't allow any of the children to do anything that might cause them or someone else to get hurt."

Fred chuckled. "As Robert and Angus found out the hard way last year, I recall. Maybe if Michael had felt your ferule, too, he wouldn't be so eager to challenge Solly. I'll talk to him—knock some sense into him if I have to. And I still think you should let me come and do the same with Solly."

"Not yet, Fred. If things get worse, I'll send for you. But I think he's getting better. At school anyway. What are we going to do about the Stonacres at home, though?"

"What do you mean? We can't do anything. Matthew was right when he told you we can't interfere with a man and his family. We don't even know for sure that he's abusing them."

"*I* know," Minta said.

"When you first came here, you disapproved of me, too, as I recall. You thought I was too hard on the kids, didn't you?" When she didn't answer, he continued, "I understand why you might think that, because of Edmund and all, but you can't go accusing people based on what you think might be happening."

"I'm not imagining the bruises and welts I see."

"No, but injuries happen in other ways, too. Kids are always hurting themselves. If Claudia and I had to account for every bruise our kids got, we wouldn't have time to do anything else."

Minta stood up abruptly. "Have you *met* Mr. Stonacre, Fred? Talked to him? He's so much like Edmund! It makes me sick to my stomach to think what he might be doing to those kids and his wife. I'm *not* imaging things!" She went to the window and folded her arms, looking out. She felt Fred come stand behind her.

"Of course I've met him. We all tried to be friendly when they first moved here. But he made it clear he didn't want to do any socializing. We've left him alone since then."

She turned to look at Fred. "Yes. That's what men like that count on—being left alone. The more isolated he can keep his family, the easier it is for him to do whatever he wants—and get away with it."

"Hmm. You're right, Minta. I hadn't thought of it that way. I'll have to think on this some more."

"And Fred, talk to Claudia. She's very wise about people. You hired me to take care of the children in this valley. I'm trying to do that. The Stonacres are almost half my children, after all. Maybe if we all work together, we can come up with a solution. I just know we can't ignore the problem."

After Fred left, Minta was feeling more hopeful about the Stonacres than she had in several days. Fred had at least agreed to think about the problem. Her grandmother always told her that a burden shared was a burden lessened. Minta was singing "Amazing Grace" as she washed the blackboards, so she didn't hear anyone come in until a polite cough caught her attention. She stopped singing and spun around.

"Silas! You gave me a start."

"I guess you're not putting a chair under the doorknob all the time any more, then?" he asked.

"No, I guess not. I did for a long time, and at night I still do. Most of the time I feel safe here, though. I still see you once in a while at night guarding the valley. I'm surprised you still keep it up every night."

"There's six of us now, doing it in rotation—me and Richard, Fred, Paulo, Jens and Ernst. If we could get Sol Stonacre to join in, we'd each only have to do it once a week. It's not that bad. I kind of like the peacefulness of the valley at night. And we want to keep it that way."

"You don't have to do it at all, Silas. As I said, I feel safer now. I've got the bell to ring if I need to. Besides, Edmund would find a way around you if he tried to come back."

"We can make it that much harder for him." Silas took off his hat and held it dangling from one hand. "And be that much closer to you if you need our help." He looked as if he were going to get closer to her to emphasize his point.

"Did you come for something, Silas?" she asked quickly.

"Oh, yeah. Here's some mail for you. I was on my way back from Halpern and seen you got something in your can." He pulled an envelope out of his back pocket.

"Thank you," Minta said, taking it. "My mother writes at least once a week now."

"I figured it was from her," Silas said, shifting from one foot to the other. "I'm glad you can write to her now. It's hard being separated from your mother, even when you grow up."

Minta set the letter on the desk and waited for him to go so she could read it. He held his cowboy hat loosely in one hand and showed no signs of leaving. She wasn't going to encourage him by offering him a seat.

"I'm sure you need to get home, Silas. Thanks for stopping by."

"No, I ain't . . . aren't in any hurry. Thought maybe you'd like to take a walk down by the creek. It's right nice outside. You been cooped up all day with kids."

"I go outside with the kids, Silas. I never feel cooped up here. Don't you need to get home to your . . . woman?"

"My . . . what?"

"Wife, friend, whatever she is."

"Who told you I got a woman?"

"The children. Apparently they've seen her at your place." Minta tried to keep her voice cool and detached.

"They did, huh?"

"Yes. And that's fine with me, Silas. I told you you should find someone . . . more appropriate."

Silas laughed, hitting his leg with his hat, sending the dust flying. "Appropriate? Oh, she's appropriate all right. She's so appropriate that . . ."

Minta's eyes widened. "So, there is someone. I thought maybe they hadn't really seen . . . but, no, they were pretty clear about what they saw."

"What did they see, Minta?" Silas asked, a wicked smile on his face.

"They said she was hanging your . . . clothes . . . on the line, and then you rode over, bent down from your horse, and kissed her. So naturally, I just assumed . . .what's so funny? Stop flapping your dirty old hat around like that. I'll have to sweep the floor all over again."

"Come on, Minta. We're going on that walk. I'll tell you all about it while we walk."

"I can't be seen walking with you. What will people say?"

"Maybe they'll say they saw us walking and talking and assume that we were being . . . 'appropriate'. Or maybe they'll mind their own business, but not likely, 'round here."

"Okay, Silas. This may well be our last walk together, but I'll go along with you just to find out what you've got to say for yourself."

"It's a long story."

"I'm sure it must be. Start talking."

They walked to the creek and began picking their way downstream along the edge. Halpern Creek was very low this time of year, and they could have stepped across it in many places. Minta was in the lead. She didn't want to look at Silas's face while he told her about his new woman.

"The story starts where I left off last year at the school meeting when I told about how my name wasn't really Silas Tower but Clayton Calhoun. You remember?"

"Of course, I remember. You thought you were wanted for murder. You changed your name just like I did."

"Well, after the sheriff told me I wasn't a wanted man no more, I figured it would be safe to go back to where I used to live in eastern Wyoming to see my mother. I wrote to her, and she wrote back that my stepfather had died and that she was in pretty bad shape."

"Oh, I'm sorry, Silas. How is she?"

"Bad shape financially, I mean. He left her with a lot of debts. She was trying to hang on to their place, hoping I'd come back. She was afraid to sell it and move 'cause then I wouldn't be able to find her. I went up there in September to see what I could do to help her."

"That's good, Silas. I guess it was there you met your . . . the woman?"

"The woman. Yes. I'm getting to that. The only thing to do was sell the home place back to the bank to pay off the debts. She couldn't have kept it up by herself anyway—too much work for a woman alone."

"I'm sure she appreciated your help. Was there enough money left to get her a small place in town?"

"No, there wasn't much left."

"Then what will she do? How will she live?"

"She found a job as a caretaker—living with a couple guys on their place."

"That doesn't sound very . . ."

"What, Minta? Appropriate? It's not 'appropriate' for her to live with two men?"

"Will you stop saying 'appropriate' that way? I'm sorry I even talked to you. I guess you're not going to tell me about your new woman, so I'd better head on back." Minta turned upstream and passed Silas. His flippant attitude about such an important subject was infuriating her.

"I just did," Silas said.

"What?" Minta stopped and turned around.

"I just told you about my woman, but she's not very new. Her name's Ethyl, but I call her Mama. She hangs my clothes on the line and, once in a while, I kiss her. I hope that's 'appropriate.'" Silas grinned.

Minta grabbed his hat off his head and hit him on the shoulder with it. They were both laughing so hard they had to sit down on the grassy bank. When she got her breath back, Minta said, "That's what I get for listening to gossiping girls. How nice for your mother. And for you, Silas. I'd like to meet her."

"I'm sure you will soon. She's been busy getting the house mucked out from all the years of us bachelors living there. And she takes most of the care of Rickerts now. She took care of my stepdad until he died, too. She's got a real soft touch. Rickerts says she's an angel come down from Heaven to show him the way up there."

There were tears in Minta's eyes. She didn't pull away when Silas put his arm around her. She allowed herself to lean into him, feeling his warmth. She closed her eyes and wished she could stay in this moment forever. Well, maybe not forever, but for a long, long time— long enough that the problem of Edmund would be solved one way or another.

"So where does that leave us, Minta?" Silas asked finally. He lifted her chin so that she was looking into his blue-green eyes.

Minta sighed. "Where we've always been. Nothing has changed for me, Silas."

"There's got to be a way for us to be together, Minta. I love you."

"Oh, Silas," Minta sobbed, pulling away and jumping up. "I have to go now. Please, don't follow me." She stumbled as she struggled the rest of the way up the bank and caught herself clumsily with one hand, jolting her wrist painfully.

"That's right," Silas said to her retreating back, "run away like you always do."

CHAPTER EIGHT

Sari's New Man

༭ﾟﾟﾟﾟﾟﾟﾟﾟﾟﾟﾟﾟﾟﾟﾟ

Devil's Creek Missouri, October 1920

Sari looked out across the field to where Eddie was working. The place sure looked nice now that he got it all fixed up. Even her chickens were laying more eggs now, and she had enough to sell in town. She kept her egg money hidden in a jar behind the mint jelly on the pantry shelf in the basement. She didn't know what she was saving it for, but felt better knowing she had a little tucked away.

Maybe she was saving it for Orville. Maybe he'd come back. He ran away a month ago, and there had been no word from him. She hadn't been surprised to get up one day and find him gone. He and Eddie never could get along. Even before Eddie came, Orville had been talking about leaving "this dump," as he called it. Young men always thought the grass was greener somewheres else. She had felt him growing away from her for a long time. That's why she needed Eddie.

Sari sighed and rubbed her back. Her back always hurt during her monthly curse—another month without a child on the way. She guessed her eggs was just getting too old, but she wouldn't tell Eddie that. She needed to keep Eddie here. He seemed to want a child as much as she did; he sure worked hard at trying to make one. She smiled. Eddie wanted her for something, anyway.

He was coming back to the house, and she went into the kitchen to get him a drink and a slice of fresh bread slathered with butter—his favorite snack.

He took it without thanks, biting off half the slice in the first mouthful.

"Pasture's lookin' good," Sari said. "Putting the cow and pig droppings on it like you done perked it right up."

"Um," Eddie mumbled with his mouth full. He drained the milk glass and handed it to her. "Just common sense to use what you got. You taking more eggs into town today?" he asked.

"Thought I might," Sari said. "You want to come along?"

"No. Just thinking we need to be saving us up some more money. Don't be spending any of it in town. Bring it all home."

"What for?" Sari asked. So he knew about the money. She'd found it very hard to keep anything from him.

"I'm planning a trip in a few months—whenever we get enough saved up."

"A trip? Where? Back wheres you used to live?"

"No, not there. You'll find out when it's time for you to know." He turned his back to her. She knew he wouldn't tell her any more until he was ready. And it would make him mad if she asked.

But he did tell her more. "Got a score to settle with someone," he said. He smiled in that way that sent chills up her back, and his eyes looked far away as if he was seeing something she couldn't. From the look on his face, and the hard lines around his eyes, she didn't *want* to see whatever it was. There was some things about Eddie—well, it was just better not knowing.

CHAPTER NINE

Ding Dong
❧✿❧

Monday, November 8, 1920, Rockytop—*Richard and Sally Mae's wedding Saturday was pleasant. It was so nice to be back at Halpern Methodist and see so many old friends. Luke Woods brought his two children and Honor, of course. It was nice to see Florence and Wendell Woods again; they've grown so and seem to be thriving in their Durango school. Silas stood up as Best Man, and Sally Mae's sister was Maid of Honor. I played several new pieces I learned this summer at the Posts' as well as the Wedding March. Richard was so nervous he could hardly repeat the words after Reverend MacIntosch. Sally Mae was more composed. She's a sturdy girl—good farm wife stock, as my father would say. Her mother cried during the whole ceremony, and I'm not sure they were tears of joy. Claudia wasn't at all tearful. It must be strange marrying off one child just a few weeks before giving birth to another. I'm continually struck by the cycles of life here—like the seasons, births and weddings and deaths keep coming around.*

Just like Christmas, which is fast approaching. The puppets are all made and we're into rehearsals now. I'll have the boys hang a rope across the classroom part way up the wall for a sheet to hide the puppeteers. The students will hold the puppets on their sticks up above the sheet. Everyone has at least one puppet, what with the Holy Family, all the Wise Men, angels, shepherds, sheep, and camels. Angus even fixed Clara's Mary puppet so it can pick up and hold Baby Jesus. I'm so proud of the creativity and work of the children. This project has really made them work together and appreciate each other's skills.

Except for Michael and Solly—they have yet to develop an appreciation for each other. I fear the only thing that has kept them from coming to blows is Fred's having threatened Michael to within an inch of his life if he gets into any fights at school, which made Michael mad at me, since he thinks I told on him. So far, I'm compensating by having the two boys at opposite ends of the stage. It wouldn't do to have Solly's camel attacking Michael's sheep or vice versa during the performance. That would make for a memorable Christmas program. Peace on Earth. At least I can laugh about it.

Minta threw herself into the day with her usual energy and enthusiasm. At noon recess she stayed inside to work on the afternoon's lessons. Angus had developed an interest in his studies for the Eighth Grade Exam, having finally decided he didn't want Michael, and especially Mary, to get ahead of him in school. He was ready for some more difficult math that Minta was preparing for him to work on after recess.

Suddenly a loud clanging noise caused her to jump to her feet. She'd never heard the bell from inside the building before. What could be wrong? She ran out the front door and almost bowled over little Dennis Stonacre who was gleefully ringing the bell and shouting, "Ding-dong, ding-dong!"

Minta pulled him away from the rope. "Dennis, what is it? What's wrong?"

"Ding-dong," Dennis replied.

Minta looked up, and the rest of the children were running toward them. "What happened?" Minta shouted. "Is someone hurt?" They all looked around at each other as she quickly counted heads: all present and breathing. She turned back to Dennis. "Why did you ring the bell, Dennis?"

He suddenly seemed to realize he was the center of attention and hung his head, reaching out for Clara, who refused to take his hand. "Answer Teacher, Dennis," Clara said, hands on her hips.

"Dunno," he mumbled into his shirt.

"Look!" Gunny shouted. "Everyone's coming!"

Minta looked up with dismay and saw three sets of dust trails, one from the east, one from the west, and the other from the south. "Oh,

Dennis, what have you done?" He started to cry and hid behind her, pulling on her skirt with his grimy hands.

Fred Haley got there first, jumping off his horse before it came to a stop. "What's wrong, Minta? Do I need to ride for the doctor?"

She shook her head. "Nothing, Fred. I'll wait and explain once everyone's here."

"Nothing!" he exploded in disgust. "It better not be nothing to get us all here!"

The last to arrive, because he had the farthest to come, was Silas. He had a gun. "Is it Edmund?" he asked. The hand holding the gun was shaking.

"No, it's not," Fred said. "Well, Minta, you'd better start explaining."

"Your parents aren't here yet, Eleanor," Gertie pointed out.

"Doubt they's coming," Clara said.

Minta explained what had happened, Dennis sniffling and holding on to her skirt behind her with one hand, the other fist stuck in his mouth. "I'm sorry, Fred," she added. "I've never talked to the children about what the bell means or made a rule about not touching it. I guess I just assumed you had, like you did about not climbing Rockytop and staying away from the creek. I'm sorry," she said again. "I'll do that now."

"I would think so." Fred glowered at her. "In the meantime, this boy is in need of a good hide-tanning. Would you like me to . . ."

"I'll take care of it, Fred," Minta said. She knew he would interpret her words differently than she meant them. She'd gotten good last year at twisting words to have the desired effect on the school board. It wasn't really lying, she rationalized. "Everyone inside now," she said to the students. "I'm sorry you all had to come over here. It won't happen again," she said to the assembled adults.

"See that it doesn't," Fred said by way of parting.

Silas was the last to leave, shaking his head as he remounted his horse.

The students were all seated quietly at their desks when she entered the classroom. There were only twelve desks for sixteen students, so the little ones sat two to a desk. Dennis shared with Dale who was patting him on the back as he sat with his head down on his arms to hide his tears. "Don't worry, Denny," Dale said. "She's not very mean, for a teacher."

"I want to tell you a story," Minta said. They all looked up in surprise at her pleasant tone as well as at her words. "Once there was a little boy whose job it was to watch over all the sheep for the whole village. The villagers all kept their sheep together like your families do the cattle." She could see the interest in their eyes. "He had to protect the sheep from the wolves by calling the adults if a wolf came close to the flock. If he saw a wolf, he was supposed to yell, 'Wolf! Wolf!' as loudly as he could. One day he got lonely and bored and decided to see what would happen if he yelled, 'Wolf!' So he did, and all the adults came running, only to find out there was nothing wrong. It was so exciting, the boy did it again the next day. It was really fun to watch all the villagers come running. He did it again and again. Finally, one day, a *big* wolf came and was about to eat a lamb, and the boy yelled, 'Wolf! Wolf!' but *no one came*," she paused. "Why do you think that was?"

"'Cause they were tired of coming," Mary said.

"Yeah, and they didn't believe that kid no more," Gertie said.

"*Any* more, Gertie. That's right. They were tired, and they didn't believe him. He cried 'wolf' one too many times, and no one believed him when the real wolf came."

"So did the wuff eat up the little lamb?" Dale asked, concern in his voice.

"I don't know. That's where the story ends."

"That's dumb," Gunny said. "Why does it end there? That's the exciting part."

"Because it's a fable—that's a story that's supposed to teach us something. What does it teach us, Eleanor?"

"Um. Not to yell 'wolf' unless you really see one?"

"Yes, but we don't have wolves here, so what does it teach *us*, specifically, Clara?"

"Don't ring no bell unless you have to?"

"That's right, Clara. It teaches us how dangerous it is to pretend there's danger when there's not. If we ever have to ring the bell for an emergency, we want everyone to believe us and come help us, don't we?"

"Yes'm," Clara said. "Did you hear that, Dennis? Don't go ringing that bell no more!"

"I told your parents I would make a rule about the bell, so here it is: *No one*, except me, is allowed to ring the bell. No one is even allowed to *touch* the rope. Is that clear? And it's not a Three Strikes Rule. It's a One Strike Rule. Serious punishment will occur if anyone breaks this rule."

"But what if you *can't* ring the bell?" Angus asked. "Like if you break your arms or something."

"Then I would tell someone to do it. Don't do it unless I tell you."

"But what if you couldn't talk, neither, like you broke your face, too?" Everett asked.

"If I can't ring the bell, and I can't talk, then the oldest student here is to do it. But you'd *better* make sure I'm out cold and not just asleep, because if I wake up and hear that bell, someone's in serious trouble!"

"Like Dennis," Michael said. "Are you going to tan him now?"

"Dennis didn't know what the bell meant. And we didn't have a rule about it yet, so he didn't know he was doing something wrong. I'm not going to punish him this time, but . . ."

"You told my dad you would."

"Shut up, Michael," Solly said.

"That's enough, Solly," Minta said. "Michael, I told your father I would take care of the situation, and I have. I'm sure we won't have any more trouble with the bell. Now we . . ."

"I'll bet if it had been . . ." Michael started to say.

"Michael, I'm tired of your interrupting me." Minta wrote his name on the board.

He jumped up out of his seat. "That's great! My name gets put on the board just for talking, and Dennis gets away with doing something really bad. I still think you ought to paddle him."

"*Someone* might get a paddling today, but it isn't going to be Dennis," Minta said. She turned and put an 'X' next to Michael's name. "Strike Two. Do you want to go for three?" She held the chalk poised while Michael glared at her. He didn't flinch, but neither did she. Finally, he sat down and said nothing further.

Minta was pleased that, for the most part, the rest of the week went smoothly. The Stonacres were responding to her "kind and patient teaching," as Miriam had characterized it. Even Solly was less belligerent, when he was there, which was less than half the time. But, surprisingly, when he came back, he often had kept up with the work with Clara's help.

Michael was still being difficult. He managed to get two strikes every day but always stopped short of the third one. She knew what Claudia meant when she said, "Michael knows just how far he can push. I declare, the more kids you have, the more gray hairs." Minta figured that meant the teacher would have more gray hairs than any of the mothers since she had *all* the kids. Last year Claudia had warned her that thirteen was the hardest age to deal with. "They want to be treated like adults," Claudia said, "but they act like two-year-olds. I thought Fred would kill Richard before he turned fourteen, and even Honor gave us some trouble at that age." Michael had turned thirteen recently. Angus was almost fourteen and starting to act more civilized than he had last year. "Mama said Michael's got to make the most of the next two months," Mary told Minta during recess, "since he's only the same age as Angus two months a year. The rest of the time Angus holds being older over his head."

Minta managed to put her difficulties with the boys in the back of her mind during her weekend in Liberty. She and Lulabelle were cleaning and tidying, preparing for her parents' visit. The Morgans would sleep in the Posts' upstairs bedroom where Minta had spent the summer, but spend most of their time with Lulabelle or visiting Minta at Rockytop. There they'd have her bedroom while she slept on a borrowed cot in the schoolroom.

Minta was excited and nervous about seeing them again. She knew she had hurt them badly when she left Indiana with no word and no way to communicate. Her mother's recent letters were affectionate but distant, kind of like their relationship had always been. Minta knew she had grown away from her parents during her time with Edmund and then here at Rockytop. She wasn't the same Ella Jane they were used to, and she wasn't sure they'd like Minta as well. She wanted to make a good impression so they would see that even though she'd made a mess of her life she was now straightening it out.

Lulabelle and Minta decided to make new curtains for the apartment from some of Frank's cloth. They went downstairs and picked out a cheerful print of multicolored flowers on a yellow background. When Frank came upstairs for lunch on Saturday, he asked, "Are you two still nesting? Must be about time for that baby to come."

"Oh, I hope so," Lulabelle said, "the sooner, the better!"

"Careful what you wish for," Minta said. "You wouldn't want it to be born prematurely and have health problems."

"Oh, pooh!" Lulabelle made a face at her. "When did you turn into Grandmother? 'Be careful what you wish for,'" she mimicked Minta's teacher voice.

"The older I get, and the more experiences I have, the more I find how right she was," Minta replied.

"Well, old, experienced lady, who's younger than I am, don't forget I'm going to be a mother before you. So there!"

"Lulabelle!" Frank said, shocked at her tone.

"Don't mind us, Frank," Minta said. "You should have heard us bicker when we were girls. Grandmother said that's how we both developed such good verbal skills. And, for your information, Lulabelle-dear, I have sixteen children. You may learn to care for babies before I do, but when this little one turns thirteen you'll be begging me for advice."

"No, I won't. I'll just send him to live with *you*."

"So, you've decided it's a boy, too?" Minta asked.

"No. But that's what Frank calls him all the time, so I do, too. It's easier. We may have the only girl who is known all her life as 'he.'"

"Have you decided on a name?" Minta asked.

"Yes," Frank said at the same time as Lulabelle said, "No, not really."

Minta laughed. "You two better get together on that pretty soon."

"His name's Frankie—Frank, Junior," Frank said. "And I'm going downstairs to work. Don't come raiding the store for more supplies either. I'd like to show some profit this month."

"Yes, sir, Mr. Businessman," Lulabelle said, "but aren't you forgetting something?"

Frank returned and gave her a perfunctory kiss. Minta suspected that, if she hadn't been there, it wouldn't have been so perfunctory.

Minta smiled as she thought about her visit with Frank and Lulabelle on the way back to Rockytop. It was the middle of November and still good weather. She enjoyed it but knew the farmers were bemoaning the lack of moisture. They had all agreed not to burn any of their fall leaves or weeds because of the fire danger.

She often prayed as she rode. Molly knew the way and was always anxious to get home to her stall. Minta didn't have to pay attention. She prayed for rain and lots of snow in the mountains so there would be irrigation water next spring and summer. She prayed for each of her students by name and for specific help she thought each needed, like more self-confidence for Clara and help with handling anger for Solly. She saved Michael for last. He needed a lot of prayer. But in the end she just prayed for wisdom and patience for his teacher.

As she was putting Molly back in her stall at the Haley's, Mary came running into the barn. "Aunt Claudia says for you to come in the house and meet someone," she said. "A new student you're going to have," she added.

"All right," Minta said, wondering who would be moving into the valley this time of year and where they'd live. Richard and Sally Mae had moved into the Woods' old place. There weren't any vacant cabins to be had that she knew of. Maybe the Haleys had relatives moving in with them. Where would they put anyone else? And where would she? The classroom already seemed too crowded with sixteen students. She brushed the trail dust off her skirt in anticipation of meeting new parents.

No one was in the kitchen where she was used to finding Claudia. "They're in the bedroom," Mary said. "Go on back there." She pointed the way, giggling.

"Claudia?" Minta called.

"Yes, Minta. Come on in. We're waiting for you."

Minta entered the bedroom to find Claudia sitting in one of the rockers that was usually on the porch in nice weather and by the stove in bad. She was holding a tiny bundle.

"Claudia! When did this happen? I wasn't here!"

"I know, Minta. You'd just left Friday for town when my water broke. She was born that night."

"May I hold her?" Minta asked. She took the bundle Claudia offered and looked down at the tiny, pink face and the black "Indian" hair. The baby stretched her arms and uncurled her miniature fingers. "What's her name?"

"Margaret," Claudia answered. "Margaret Minta—the kids insisted on Minta. I like it, too. But we'll call her Meg. And when it's time for the christening, we'd like you to stand up as her godmother. Would you?"

"Of course, Claudia, I'd be honored to. But who would be her god-father, since I don't have a husband . . . to speak of?"

"We kind of thought we'd ask Silas."

Dismayed, Minta thought about how to respond as she opened the blanket and inspected the tiny toes. Finally she looked up. "Oh, dear. That would mean Silas and I would have to stand up together in church. I don't know, Claudia. It might be . . . awkward."

"I'm not asking you to stand up in church and marry him, just pledge to make sure Meg gets raised a proper Christian."

"But surely there's other, more appropriate . . ." Minta stopped, remembering her last 'appropriate' conversation.

"Jens and Hannah are Judy's godparents, and Paulo and Sophie are Dale's. Rickerts is Robert's. Us and Rickerts were all who lived here when Robert was born, so he only has one godparent. The rest were born before we came here and have godparents among our families. I can't think of anyone more appropriate than you and Silas. But, if you don't want to . . ."

Minta looked down at the rosebud face again. How could she refuse? "Of course, I want to, Claudia," she said. She'd have to figure out how to deal with the problem of standing up with Silas before the time came. Silas might look on it as some kind of commitment. More than just to Meg. Other people might, too. She knew from whispered conversations she overheard at school that people were gossiping about her and Silas. Why couldn't her life be as uncomplicated as the little bundle she held in her arms? Meg opened her eyes and turned her head, looking for something to suck on. Minta quickly returned her to Claudia.

"Sit on the bed a spell, while I nurse her," Claudia said. "How was your visit in town?"

"Oh, fine. I sure hope Lulabelle's baby is born soon and that it's all right."

"Is there a reason to think it might not be?"

"No, it's just we're both so anxious about it."

"You sound like a first-time father instead of the cousin of the mother. You and Lulabelle must be very close. Don't you worry about going there as soon as you hear from her. Just let school out, or put a note on the board that you're gone. If you don't ring the bell some morning, Fred will go check on you and let everyone know if you've gone to town."

"Thank you. Matthew has promised to come get me when Lulabelle's time comes. I hope I can get there for the birth, but, if not, I want to be there as soon after as possible. She'll have the doctor, of course, but . . . Oh Claudia, I forgot. Did you have the doctor?"

"No. What would I need him for? Rachel was here, and Hannah and Sophie both came over to help. That reminds me, while they were here, we talked about the Stonacre problem."

"You, what? While you were giving birth?"

"No, silly. The next day. They stayed to make sure Meg and I were all right and to fix some food for the family."

"Of course, they would," Minta said. "Did you solve the Stonacre problem?"

"Hardly," Claudia said, "but we decided what Fred said that you said was right. Isolation is part of the problem. We can't let them isolate themselves like that."

"But how can we stop them?"

"By being good neighbors. We all agreed we'd make excuses to drop in at their place, so they never know when someone's coming."

"I'd be careful about that. If Sol thinks his wife is having women friends over, he might be . . ."

"Oh, it won't be just us. We got the men to agree to do it, too. I remember you said how Edmund was a good farmer and neighbors used to come ask him for advice. The men are going to make excuses to go talk to Sol, too—let him know that we all help each other and, more importantly, keep an eye on each other, around here. We agreed we'd all be polite and friendly, but firm. We won't take 'go away' for an answer."

"I hope it works, Claudia."

"Often the best way to get people to change their habits is to show them by example new ways. Maybe we can be examples of how we do things here. Kind of like how you teach the kids, Minta. You do your magic with them, and we'll see what we can do about the grown-ups. Speaking of kids, Michael isn't giving you trouble is he?"

"Why do you ask?" Minta said, trying to figure out an answer. She had told the kids last year she wouldn't tell on them, but if their parents asked her a direct question, she'd have to answer truthfully.

"Oh, he's just at that age," Claudia rolled her eyes. "I swear, some days he'd cut off his nose to spite his face."

"Well, I'll try to send him home each day with his nose intact. It may be out of joint, though."

"You're not answering the question, Minta."

"I know. I'd rather not."

Chapter Ten

Where Did You Come From, Baby Dear?

❧❦❧

Friday, November 26, 1920, Rockytop—*I've come to dread Fridays almost as much as the kids love them. I know it's hard for them to contain their excitement at the week's ending, but their extra energy makes my job harder. It doesn't help that we rehearse on Friday afternoons for the Christmas Program which adds to their exuberance. Today I have a poetry reading lesson planned for the morning. I think the whole school can participate because the younger ones can listen to and appreciate the poetry even if they can't read it themselves.*

Lulabelle seems to be doing better as she waits for the arrival of the little one. Claudia's little Meg is thriving in the loving Haley household. I'm so enjoying Meg and looking forward to greeting Lulabelle's baby. How exciting it must be for them! That's one of my biggest regrets—that I'll probably never be able to experience motherhood myself. I often wonder what would have happened if I'd had Edmund's child. It would have been much more difficult and dangerous to leave him. But I would have loved to have had a child. However, I thank the Lord that He didn't place me in that position. Dare I now pray for another chance with a kinder man? Grandmother said God doesn't care what I pray for or how I pray. He knows what I desire and what is best for me. I guess I'll just have to let God sort it out. I surely can't.

Minta was startled to see that it was almost time to ring the first bell. She jumped up, took off her apron, pushed a strand of hair back under its hairpin and began her day. All sixteen students were present and on time, a pleasant rarity. Rehearsal should go more smoothly with all of them there.

In fact, she felt the first part of the school year had gone as well as could be expected. Michael and Solly still looked daggers at each other but hadn't come to blows. The girls had settled down their giggling and gossiping and were starting to work on their grammar. Well, except for one day last week when she caught them out behind the outhouse talking about Richard and Sally Mae. "My mother says they're having one of those seven-month babies," Mary was saying.

"What do you mean?" Gertie asked. "Babies take nine months to come; everyone knows that."

"Sometimes the first one only takes six or seven, my mother says," Mary replied. "Like Angus. My folks were married in July, and Angus was born the next January."

Clara snickered. "Yeah, I heard of that happening, too. Usually premature babies are really little, but when folks has a 'seven-month' first baby, it ain't."

"How come?" Gertie asked.

Minta interrupted before Clara had a chance to answer. After reprimanding them about gossiping and correcting Clara's use of 'ain't,' she set them to work making up the design for the invitations to the Christmas Program.

"Be sure to tell your parents it's important for them to be here," she told the Stonacre girls.

"Yeah, we know," Clara said. "I think those ladies that come bother Ma all the time already done told her anyway." So Claudia was keeping her word about visiting the Stonacres. Minta hoped the men were being successful with Sol, too. At least none of the children had come to school injured lately—that she could *see*, anyway.

She considered what the girls had been gossiping about. That would explain why Sally Mae's mother had cried through the whole ceremony and why Claudia seemed in such a hurry to have the wedding. Last year Claudia had promised to tell her girls where babies came from before they got old enough to find out the hard way. Apparently she didn't tell her son. Minta wished more mothers would tell their children—not that her own mother had. Why was it something people found so hard to talk about? Even Minta said and thought "it" instead of "intercourse." It made her blush even to think the word to herself. Her mother had said to her, once, "I suppose you know you need a man to have babies." That had been the extent of Minta's education on the matter until her horrible wedding night with Edmund, who was neither kind nor patient, and certainly not gentle. From his crude remarks she learned how conception actually occurred.

Would it be possible to teach about such a thing in school, she wondered. No. That would be impossible. She'd have to separate the boys from the girls and find a man to teach the boys while she taught the girls. And the parents might be mad that she took it upon herself to do so. But the children shouldn't be getting their information from Clara's whispered words on the playground as they were now. They all knew about the birth of babies, thanks to their younger siblings and the farm animals. But she was sure they didn't have very accurate information about how the babies got to be inside the mothers in the first place. While preparing today's lesson, she had found a poem in the 1905 Alexander—Blake *Graded Poetry Reader* she had inherited from the Liberty School when it was cleaning out its old books. The poem was called "The Baby." It started out asking, "Where did you come from, baby dear," and then proposed a series of questions about where the baby got all of its parts (hands, toes, etc.). The answers came from the baby's point of view. The last two verses read:

> *How did they all come to be you?*
> *God thought about me, and so I grew.*
> *But how did you come to us, my dear?*
> *God thought of you, and so I am here.*

Minta could just imagine the classroom discussion that poem might generate. No, she couldn't bring up the idea of teaching that sort of thing with the school board. For one thing, they were all men. That would be too embarrassing. She knew what Fred would say, anyway: "You have enough to teach them already. Just do a good job with what you were hired to do." She'd better leave it at that. And she'd skip that stupid poem when they came to it in the reader.

The first half of the morning passed quickly with all the lessons they had to get through. After morning recess, she told the students to pull their chairs into a circle so they could read poetry together. She ignored the groans of the older boys. They seemed to think they had to object to poetry on principle. She told them to get out their *Poetry Readers* and turn to page thirty-three. She picked "Over in the Meadow" to start with because she knew the younger students would like it.

"There are ten stanzas," Minta said. "So I want each fourth through eighth grader to read one of them, starting with Mary and going around the circle. I want you first through third graders to listen very carefully, so when we're done reading you can tell me what animals were in the meadow and what they did. Okay Mary, begin." She picked Mary to start since she was the best reader. Minta hoped Mary's lilting voice would set the cadence for the rest of the readers to keep up the pace and singsong quality of the poem.

"Over in the meadow, in the sand, in the sun, lived an old mother toad and her little toady, one. 'Wink', said the mother . . ." Mary began, projecting her voice toward the little ones. She read to them quite often and knew how to keep their attention.

Things were fine until stanza nine when Solly changed "plashed" to "splashed" and was corrected by Michael. Then they had to have a discussion about whether "plashed" was a real word and whether it was all right for poets to make up words. Minta thought it was all right, even though she agreed with the students that "splashed in the sun" sounded just as good as "plashed in the sun."

The younger students were able to name all ten animals mentioned in the poem because they were all ones familiar to them—lizards, spiders, toads, bees, crows, and so forth. Gunny objected to the mother animals speaking English to their babies because "critters don't talk words," so a discussion of personification was in order. They finally finished that poem and were ready to go on to another.

"Let's skip over to page thirty-nine and look at Tennyson's poem," Minta said.

"Why do we got to skip?" Eleanor asked. "I want to read the baby one."

"Yeah, me too," Gertie said, always ready to agree with Eleanor. "I like babies."

Minta sighed. She couldn't very well explain her reasons for skipping it. "It has some difficult vocabulary," she said. "Clara, why don't you read it to us?" Maybe Clara's dull voice and the words they didn't know would distract the students from the poem's message.

"Where did you come from, baby dear? Out of the everywhere into the here," Clara started.

"That's dumb," Michael said. "What does that even *mean*?"

"Michael, don't interrupt," Minta said. "And we've discussed before that you don't make judgments like 'dumb' or 'stupid' about literature. If you have an objection, state it in quantifiable terms. Go on, Clara."

"Where did you get your eyes so blue? Out of the sky as I came through. What makes the light in them sparkle and spin? Some of the starry spikes left in."

Dennis gasped. "Does that baby got spikes in its eye? How come? Don't that hurt?"

Minta wished she were dealing with adults. Then she'd say something about taking the plank out of your own eye before you worry about the spikes in the baby's. She was really close to agreeing with Michael's assessment of the poem as "dumb."

"It's just a word picture, Dennis," Mary explained. "The baby's eyes are supposed to look like stars. Let's let Clara read the whole thing, okay?"

Clara managed to get to the lines "Where did you get that pearly ear? God spoke, and it came out to hear" before the room erupted with the laughter of the older boys.

"Can't you just see that?" Robert said. "The ear just pops out of the head like . . . like . . . blowing a piece of that Blibber Blubber gum we got at the Fair last year."

"Okay," Minta said. "I can see you're not going to take this poem seriously, so we might just as well . . ."

"We take it seriously," Mary said. "I want to know how it ends. Please finish, Clara."

Minta fixed the boys with her 'look', as they called it, and they quieted down while Clara finished reading. "God thought about me, and so I grew. But how did you come to us, my dear? God thought about you, and so I am here."

"All right," Minta said. "We read the poem. Now let's . . ."

"We have to discuss it," Gertie said. "Does it mean God thinks about a baby and that's how it gets in the mother's tummy?"

"Yes," Minta said. "Now let's turn to . . ."

"I object to this poem on the grounds it's not accurate," Michael said. "God doesn't think babies inside mothers."

"I don't think we can presume to say we know what God does or doesn't think, Michael," Minta said.

"Then how come the poem says God thinks that?" Robert asked. "Can the poet man *presume* to know what God thinks, but we can't?"

"If God thinks about putting babies in certain mothers, how come He puts so many in some, like Eleanor's Ma, and not any in others who really, really want babies? Doesn't He care if they want them or not?" Gertie asked.

"I don't think Ma wanted the last two," Everett said. "I know I didn't."

"And how come he makes some babies that aren't right, like Joseph Valori?" Gunny asked.

"We love Joseph!" Paul defended his disabled little brother.

"I know you do, but I still don't get why God would let a kid be messed up like that," Gunny said.

"I think these are questions you should ask Reverend MacIntosch or your parents," Minta said. "I'm not going to try to answer them. I don't know the answers."

"You don't know where babies come from?" Michael asked.

"That wasn't one of the questions," Minta said.

"Okay, where do . . ." Michael started as Angus kicked the side of his leg with the toe of his boot. "Ouch!" Michael retaliated by punching Angus on the arm which pushed him into Solly who slid off his chair onto the floor to the delight of the younger boys. Before Minta could react, Solly jumped up, pulled Michael out of his chair, and raised his fist.

Minta stood and pushed her way in-between them, facing Solly. She was pretty sure Michael wouldn't hit her, but wasn't as sure about Solly. She placed her hands on his shoulders and looked him in the eye. "Stop it, right now."

Angus stood up, too. "I'm sorry," he said. "I started it. If you're going to punish someone, it should be me."

"Mary and Clara," Minta said. "Take everyone else outside for one game of Red Rover. You three boys stay here."

After the rest of the children were outside, Minta sat Angus, Michael, and Solly in three chairs facing her.

"Okay, Angus. Why did you kick Michael?"

"Because he was going to ask you where babies come from, and I knew you didn't want to answer."

"How gallant," Michael said sarcastically.

"You don't need to protect me, Angus," Minta said.

"Yes, ma'am. Sorry. I won't do it again."

"Michael, why did you hit Angus?" Minta asked.

"'Cause he kicked me."

"Solly, why did you try to hit Michael?"

"'Cause he made Angus knock me down."

"Do you all hear how stupid you sound?" Minta asked.

"How come you can say we're stupid, but we can't say that poem is stupid?" Michael asked.

Minta threw up her hands. "The poem IS stupid. Whoever put it in that book is stupid. This whole stupid discussion is stupid!"

They were all three staring at her with wide eyes. "Are you all right?" Angus asked.

Minta couldn't help laughing at their expressions. They must think she'd taken leave of her senses. Well, she had, but only temporarily. She got her face under control and looked at them sternly.

"Angus, your punishment is to write a poem about the stupidity of fighting. Michael, yours is to write one about the stupidity of sarcasm. And, Solly, I want you to write a poem about self-control. You will stand and read them to the class first thing tomorrow morning."

"But . . ." Solly started to say. She ignored him as she called the rest of the students back in.

Chapter Eleven

Double Trouble

Tuesday, December 21, 1920, Rockytop—*I'm trying to write quietly so as not to wake my parents. They arrived with the Posts last night just in time for the Christmas program, so I didn't have time to greet them properly until afterwards. Then we stayed up half the night talking. It's hard to believe I haven't seen them since many months before I ran away from Edmund—almost two years. I feel as if I've changed a great deal in that time, but they haven't. Mother is still quiet and stoic, what I used to think of as disapproval of me rather than just her nature. Father is still calm and detached. I'm ashamed to say that as a teenager I went through a stage where I used to do things just to try to get some sort of reaction out of them. After waiting twenty years to have a child, they were so set in their ways that, for me, living in their house was like trying to be a miniature adult. I was more than ready to go on to college after graduating from high school a year early. And, I thought, ready to be married. Now I know I wasn't ready. Maybe to a different man, a man like Silas. No. I can't start thinking along those lines.*

I'm so glad my parents got here in time for the program, and Lulabelle and Frank were able to come, too. I know it's vain to want to show off, but I wanted my parents to see my students and the school at their best. Lulabelle wasn't going to come because Grandmother always said women shouldn't show themselves in that condition, but I convinced her no one at Rockytop would care. I told her Alice Fredrickson came to last year's Christmas program just two weeks before her baby was born, and she had to sit sideways in the desk to fit. I pointed out to Lulabelle that she isn't nearly as large as Alice was. In fact, in her bulky winter clothing most people wouldn't even notice she was with child.

The program went pretty well. The puppets and the kids were cute, so no one really minded that they couldn't hear Dennis and Beth or that Gina forgot some of her lines. The best performance was the duet Clara and Mary sang. I had no idea Clara was an alto until I started giving them music lessons. The two harmonize beautifully. Mary also played a simple song on the piano. Everyone admired the puppets after the show and were very impressed with Eleanor's sewing and the boys' carving and painting abilities. Even the Stonacre parents showed up. They came late and sat in the back. I imagine their children badgered them into it. I hope they were proud of their kids' efforts, even though they left early and didn't stay to speak to me.

Silas was Santa again this year, but I think people figured it out. Mr. Rickerts came to the program, too, although he had to be carried in and out. I'm afraid he isn't long for this world. Silas said he told them he wouldn't miss the Christmas program unless he was "six feet under being worm vittles." Oh! I finally got to meet Silas's mother, Ethyl. She seemed nice, but we really didn't get to talk. She was busy tending to Mr. Rickerts, trying to keep him comfortable. She just said, "So you're the one," whatever that means. I knew better than to ask. Mr. Rickerts even insisted on drinking a cup of the spiced cider over Ethyl's protestations about what it would do to his insides. "Gol durn it, woman," he said. "Quit your fussin'. If it kills me, you can say 'I told you so' over my grave." Then he turned to me and said, "And ask them two purdy girls what sang so sweet tonight to sing at my grave, too." Now I know what Grandmother meant when she said someone acted like he had one foot in the grave.

Minta got up to pour herself a cup of coffee and walked over to the window with it. Still no snow. It had turned cold and windy, but the sky was as cloudless as ever. It made it easier for everyone going back and forth to Liberty but wasn't what they needed for the farms. She enjoyed the luxury of enjoying her coffee with no school or students to plan for. School would be closed now until sometime in January.

She smiled as she thought of her students and the challenge they brought to her days. They certainly kept her too busy to fret about her problems. Not that they didn't cause many problems of their own. Although, they'd been remarkably good the last two weeks, the older boys reminding them often that they'd have to write punishment poems if they misbehaved. No one seemed to want to repeat the performances of the three boys who'd had to recite their poems to the class.

Minta almost laughed out loud as she remembered the poems. Angus had gone first, standing red-faced as he recited "Fighting is dumb, like drinking rum. They both make you look like a fool. So take my advice. Put your anger on ice, and you won't get in trouble at school." That actually wasn't too bad poetically, unlike Michael's, which was on the verge of being insubordinate: "Sarcasm is Stupid is the name of my poem. But nothing rhymes with either. Except cupid which doesn't make sense. So my poem is stupid and doesn't rhyme and I sarcastically couldn't care less." She had been afraid Solly would refuse to do it at all, but he stood in front of the class and read off of a grimy piece of paper: "Self control is good. It keeps you outa trubble. So do what you should, or you'll get in trubble dubble."

Minta had almost gotten in double trouble, too. The day after the poetry reading fiasco, all three members of the school board showed up to talk to her after school. They had heard that she had been having discussions with the students about where babies came from and that there had been a fight in the classroom.

"I know we need to hear your side of it first," Fred said. "The kids often don't give us the whole story," he explained to Jens and Paulo.

Minta sighed and tried to explain how the discussion of the poem had degenerated to the point where the older boys almost got into a fight. She could tell that Jens and Paulo thought the whole situation humorous, but Fred's face turned red in anger as she described the misbehavior of his son and nephew.

"I've already punished them, Fred," she said. "I hope you don't feel it necessary to add to it."

"I don't call writing poems punishment," Fred said. "You *know* what I'd do."

"Actually, I think the boys would have preferred corporal punishment. It would have been over much more quickly and been less embarrassing."

"She's right, Fred," Jen's said. "My two are terrified of maybe having to write a poem now."

"The children *do* need some accurate information about where babies come from," Minta said. "I understand you don't want me to provide that at school, so you need to make sure they get it at home." She hesitated. Dare she ask them? "When and where did you learn about, you know, the facts of life?" she finally asked the men, her face turning red.

They all three looked as uncomfortable as she felt. "High school biology maybe?" Paulo finally answered. "I know we learned how mammals conceive and give birth. And we learned people are mammals. I think we were just supposed to figure it out from there."

"I never went to high school," Fred said. "I think I learned from other kids—you know, just talking at recess."

"And was the information you got from other kids accurate?" Minta asked.

"Some of it. But it wasn't very . . . nicely put, I guess I'm trying to say."

"Exactly," Minta said. "They need accurate information, and they need it to be nicely put."

"You're right, as usual, Minta. I'll talk to Claudia about it," Fred said. "We'll make sure our kids know what's what."

The others agreed to talk to their wives, too. At least half of her students would be well-informed now. There was still the Stonacre problem. Minta wished her parents had been more forthcoming with her.

Minta was jolted back to the present by hearing her parents stirring in the bedroom. They had decided to spend a relaxing day at Rockytop visiting with her since they hadn't been able to do so in the last two years. Then they would all go into Liberty tomorrow to visit with Posts and Lulabelle and Frank. After their morning trip to the outhouses, her parents joined her by the stove for a cup of coffee. Minta usually just had oatmeal for breakfast, but today she had decided to cook some of the Haley's eggs and make pancakes. Her mother took over making the pancakes as Minta fried the eggs.

"I don't think I ever had breakfast in a schoolroom," her father said, looking around. "Plenty of lunches, but not breakfast. There was that one time we got snowed in at school. Course all there was for breakfast the next morning was some dry bread the teacher had and melted snow water."

"How interesting," Minta said. "You've never told me much about your school days."

"Well, this little school of yours brings back a lot of memories. Just the smell of the chalk makes me feel forty years younger."

"More like fifty," her mother said dryly. "I never thought I'd see our daughter teaching at a one-room school, though. Land sakes, all the schools back home are at least four-room now."

"I like it," Minta said. "It's just the right size for me. And I like not having other teachers around questioning how I do things."

"Why is that?" her mother asked. "Don't you do things like you're supposed to?" She fixed Minta with her perceptive eye, the one Minta knew would show if she were being truthful. Her mother's salt and pepper hair had already started to escape its bun. It seldom lasted until noontime, and she usually just gave up and tied a scarf around it.

"I try to do what I'm supposed to," Minta said. "Fred thinks I'm not strict enough. I can't seem to convince people that there's more than one way to discipline children. And there are a lot of things I'd like to teach that aren't on the state curriculum. There's never enough time to do all I want to do."

Her father chuckled. "That sounds like you. There was never enough time to do all you wanted as a kid, either. Remember when you and Lulabelle decided to build a tree house? I was willing to help you build a platform, but you wanted a real house, with a roof and glass windows and I don't remember what all."

"She probably would have done it all, too, if she hadn't fallen out of the tree and broken her arm," her mother said.

"That was the summer I got so close to Grandmother," Minta said. "She sat and read and talked to me while my arm healed."

"I never did understand how you fell out of that tree," her father said. "That platform we built was plenty big and sturdy to hold you two girls."

Minta smiled. "I promised Lulabelle I wouldn't tell, but I guess I can now. We were Indian wrestling up there. She pulled my arm a little too hard, and I went over the edge."

"Lulabelle *was* bigger and stronger than you back then," her mother said. "You kept challenging her to Indian wrestle because you just knew one day you'd come out on top. But I never imagined you'd do anything like that up in a tree!"

"Well, kids do some dumb things," Minta said. "I'm reminded of that almost every day in school. It's a wonder any of us live to grow up."

They sat down in three of the desks to eat, a companionable silence enveloping them. Minta sighed in contentment. It had been awkward at first, but she was beginning to feel comfortable around them again. They'd forgiven Ella Jane for running off without telling them where she'd gone and were willing to accept her now, as Minta. They were beginning to treat her less like the young girl she had been and more like an adult. It would take all three of them time to adjust to their new relationship.

After breakfast Minta was anxious to show her parents all she'd done with the school and her lessons—the bedroom curtains she'd made and the lesson plans she carefully wrote out a week in advance. Of course, she didn't always stick with them, but at least she started each week well organized.

If it warmed up some, she might even take them part way up Rockytop to enjoy the view of the valley and see where everyone lived.

As she cleaned up the breakfast dishes, she contemplated her plans for the day until she heard someone arriving on horseback. She looked out the window to see Richard. She stepped outside to greet him. "Hello, Richard. What brings you around so early?"

"It's Old Man Rickerts. He died last night. Guess the trip to the program was too much for him. Silas asked me to let everyone know."

"Poor Silas! Should we ring the bell?"

"No. It's not an emergency. I'll just ride around and tell folks. He already had his services planned. He just wants to be buried on his place—the upper pasture with the good view. He said he didn't want a bunch of wailing and churchgoing, just some words over the open grave. Silas says they'll do it tomorrow afternoon at two. He especially asked if you'd be there. Rickerts was right fond of you."

"Of course I'll be there," Minta said. "And I'll go pay my respects to Silas and his mother today. I know Silas was very fond of Mr. Rickerts, too." Richard had started to ride away when Minta called him back. "I just remembered something Mr. Rickerts said last night. He wanted Mary and Clara to sing at his grave. Would you tell them when you call on their families? The only song they've learned together besides the Christmas one is 'The Old Rugged Cross.' That should do."

When Minta went back inside, her parents were finishing up the coffee. "I'm afraid our plans for today and tomorrow have changed," she told them. She explained about the death and funeral.

"Of course, you must go do what you need to do, Minta. Don't worry about us," her father said.

"Why don't you two go ahead and take Matthew's buggy back to Liberty today?" Minta said. "They won't mind you coming a day early and without me. There will be more for you to do in town than sitting around an empty school. I'll join you after the funeral."

"How will you get there?" her mother asked.

"I'll borrow Molly and ride her like I've been doing most weekends. But can you find your way back by yourselves?" She turned to her father.

"We just go back down the road we came up on until we get to that little church, turn right, and take that road into Liberty, correct?"

"That's right. Turn right at Halpern and just follow the road."

"I think we can manage, Minta. We did survive the last two years on our own."

Minta laughed. "I know you did. And I know you have a good sense of direction, Dad. I'm just sorry I can't go with you as we planned."

"We'll stay here until you go to visit the bereaved this afternoon," her mother said. "But then I would like to get back to Lulabelle. Seeing that little Margaret Minta baby last night made me even more anxious for Lulabelle's to get here. I feel like I'm going to be a grandmother, finally."

"You almost are," Minta said. "I'm sure Lulabelle will welcome your grandmotherly administrations. I'm sorry I haven't provided you with any grandchildren."

"Oh, I didn't mean that, El . . . Minta. I just meant that I was as old as many grandmothers when I had you. It's past time I *was* one, but that's not your fault. I'm glad you didn't have any children with that horrible man."

"No. I'd still be tied to him. Even more than I am, I mean," Minta turned her back so they wouldn't see the tears that had sprung to her eyes.

"You *could* get a divorce," her mother said.

"Mother! You know I'd never do that. I don't believe in divorce."

"Sometimes I wish we were Catholic. Then maybe you could get the marriage annulled."

"I doubt it," Minta said. "Not from what I've heard about the reasons for annulment. And you're the one who taught me divorce was wrong. Why are you changing your mind now?"

"I just don't want to see you spending your life living like an old maid."

"What she means is she wants grandchildren," her father said. "More than Lulabelle's almost ones. Funny how a woman can change her mind when she wants something bad enough."

"Well, I can't," Minta said. "And I don't want to talk about it any more. Come see how I've arranged the desks and materials for my reading groups."

She spent the rest of the morning showing her parents around the school and where the teacherage had been. Then they went up Rockytop far enough to be able to see where the Haleys, Valoris, and Fredricksons lived. "The valley is so much prettier in any season other than winter. I wish you could see it in the spring when everything's newly green," she said. "Or the fall! That's my favorite time. Those cottonwoods down along the creek make a ribbon of gold, and the oak brush on this hillside here turns all different colors of red and orange and yellow. It looks like someone threw a calico quilt over the hill."

"Sounds like you really love it here." Her father looked up at the rocks topping the small mountain. "Have you been all the way up there?" he asked.

"Oh, yes, many times," she answered. "In nice weather, it's a wonderful place to sit with my books and . . ."

"Daydream? Like you used to spend all your time doing, if I didn't find you and put you to work?" her mother asked.

"Not daydream, really. But it is a good place to think. God puts the world into perspective for me there."

Her father shook his head. "What a thing to say. When did you get so . . . deep?"

Minta thought about all the events of the past year that had changed her. In some ways she still felt like her parents' child, but in others she was a million miles from them and their shared experiences. She couldn't explain all that to her father.

She went back to an easier topic. "There is a flat rock up on Rockytop I like to sit on. It's right next to a big drop-off on the other side. You can't see the drop-off until you're right up next to it. I like to look over the edge at the tops of the piñon and juniper trees far below. And I like to look this way, over the valley and all the homes of my students. I kind of feel like I'm surveying my world up there."

"Your world," her father said. "Yes, darling, I guess this is your world now. And from all the nice comments we heard at the Christmas program, the people here think of you as theirs, too."

A cold gust of wind reminded them that it was winter, driving them back down the slope and inside.

After they made themselves a light lunch, she saw her parents off to Liberty and got herself ready to go borrow Molly and to visit Silas. She realized she'd never been all the way to his place. She knew it was the next one after the Archu . . . Stonacres', but that's as far south as she'd been on the Piñon Hollow Road.

Silas and his mother were receiving people in the livingroom. Richard was there, as well as Hannah and Jens Fredrickson. Ethyl insisted on fixing Minta a cup of tea and passed around a plate of cookies that Hannah had brought. Minta mentally kicked herself for not thinking to bring food. She should know by now that you always brought food when visiting a family in mourning.

She sat down across from Silas who looked drained—like he hadn't slept for a long time. "I'm so sorry, Silas," she said. "I know how much he meant to you."

"If it weren't for him, I wouldn't . . ." Silas' voice broke.

"I know, Silas. But at least you didn't have to take him out to the pasture and shoot him."

Ethyl gasped.

"It's okay, Mom," Silas said. "That's what he told me to do when he got too old and hard to take care of. Maybe I would have, if you hadn't been here to help."

"Clayton Calhoun! What a thing to say!"

"Just kidding, Mom. Minta reminded me that humor is a good way to handle problems. You got to be able to laugh at yourself."

"Yes, that's right," Hannah said. "You can't take yourself too seriously. That's what the kids love about Minta, too. She makes them laugh at themselves instead of getting upset when they make mistakes."

Minta was embarrassed. This wasn't supposed to be about her. She turned to Silas' mother. "I'm sorry I didn't get to talk to you at the program, Mrs. . . . Calhoun?"

"No. Calhoun was my first husband, Clay . . . Silas' father. I remarried after he died. Call me Ethyl."

"How do you like our little valley?" Hannah asked.

"Oh, it's fine. I haven't been out much—taking care of . . . you know. I guess I'll have time now to get out and meet people. The Christmas program was really the first social thing I've been to since I got here."

"Yeah. I've been keeping her prisoner here—slave labor, you know," Silas said.

"Oh you!" His mother slapped him on the leg. "Behave yourself!"

"I know you've been a big help to Silas since you came," Minta said. "He needed a woman on the place to . . ." She stopped, realizing her mistake.

"Yes, that's what he's been telling me, too. He needs a woman. He seems to think he found one." She frowned at Minta. Minta knew Silas must have told his mother about his attempts to court her. She thought she knew what his mother was thinking—Minta wasn't an appropriate match for her only son. That is, if Silas had told her Minta was still married. He must have, the way his mother was frowning at her. Well, if that's what she was thinking, she was right. Minta wasn't an appropriate match for Silas. Everyone, except Silas, seemed to be able to grasp that fact.

In the awkward silence, as Minta stared at her lap, the Fredricksons got up to leave. Richard walked out the door with them to talk to Jens. Minta didn't want to be alone with Silas and his mother, but didn't know of a polite way to extricate herself. She took a long, slow sip of tea and nibbled on the cookie that was beginning to crumble in her hand.

"Aren't your parents here?" Silas asked her.

"No. I sent them into town today. I'll join them after . . . tomorrow. You did say two o'clock, didn't you?" She stood to take her leave. "I'll return then. Oh! I told Richard to ask Mary and Clara to sing tomorrow. I hope that's all right with you."

"That would be very nice," Ethyl said. "I heard what the old man said to you. Thoughtful of you to make it happen."

"Yes, Minta's always thoughtful. And she tends to make things happen," Silas said, standing to walk outside with her.

The Fredricksons were gone, but Richard was leaning on the porch post. "You don't have to stay all day," Silas said to him. "I thank you for coming, but Sally Mae might need you."

"No, she's fine," Richard said. "I said I'd stay with you, and I will."

"That's kind of you, Richard. Silas is lucky to have such a good friend," Minta said.

"I'm the one that's lucky. There aren't any guys my age in the valley, and all the men are as old as my father except Ernst, but he acts as old. Until Silas came, I felt like a loner. He's been a good friend to me. Helped me figure out what to do when Sally Mae told me . . ." He stopped, embarrassed.

"Told you she was in the family way?" Minta asked gently.

"Yeah. I guess we jumped the gun a little. You should have heard my father yelling."

"I can imagine," Minta said. "I know Fred."

"I came over and talked to Silas, and he helped me figure out how to make it all work out. He said if I loved Sally Mae enough to get her in that condition, I should be her husband. Seems like I've always wanted to do the opposite of what my father told me to do, but when Silas said the same thing, it seemed to make more sense. And now that I'm out of my folks' place and on my own—well, kind of on my own, I still farm with my father—I'm starting to get along better with him. I owe that to Silas."

"Yes, I've found it's good to share your burdens. Often other people can help you figure out what to do when you're stymied," Minta said.

Silas took her hand and helped her mount Molly. "Thanks for coming, Minta. Now that you know where I live, don't be a stranger."

Minta looked at Richard. She knew what Silas was asking but couldn't really say anything in front of a third party. "I'll see you tomorrow, Silas."

"That's not the same. Everybody will be here. When can I see you alone?"

"Silas, please, not in front of . . ."

"Richard knows how I feel. I have burdens to share, too, you know."

CHAPTER TWELVE

Two Birthdays

❦

Tuesday, January 4th, 1921, Liberty—Happy birthday to me! I can't believe I'm twenty-one and I get to spend the day with my family. I almost didn't get to spend Christmas with them. The cold wind that had been blowing the day they arrived brought in storm clouds. It started snowing during Rickerts' funeral, and I was unable to get to town for several days. I did manage to get here just in time to celebrate Christmas in Lulabelle's little apartment.

I haven't written about the funeral yet. I wanted some time before I tried. I liked Reverend MacIntosch's choice of the first chapter of Second Corinthians for the text, especially these verses:

"Blessed be God, even the Father of our Lord Jesus Christ, the Father of mercies, and the God of all comfort; Who comforteth us in all our tribulation, that we may be able to comfort them which are in any trouble, by the comfort wherewith we ourselves are comforted of God."

I felt such comfort by the company of those present, as I hope Silas did. When the preacher asked any of us who wanted to say something to come forward, I was afraid Silas wouldn't be able to manage. But he spoke first about how Mr. Rickerts became a second father to him. Ethyl talked about how she'd grown to love him and how grateful she was to him for "saving" her son from "life as a fugitive," as she put it. I spoke about how much Mr. Rickerts enjoyed all the school events and how his serving as Santa all those years meant a lot to the children. I was surprised when Robert came forward to speak until I remembered he was the godson. It's funny how in life we all called him Old Man Rickerts, but in death none of us did. Robert said, "Mr. Rickerts was a good man. Last year he gave our school a new ball and bat. I talked to the other kids and we're going to dedicate this year's softball tournament game to him." I'm sure the "old man" was smiling down from heaven and will be in attendance at that event. Even without piano accompaniment, Clara and Mary sang beautifully, as I knew they would, and I saw many a tear shed. Clara was the only one of her family in attendance, but at least they allowed her to come.

Just as they finished singing, the snow started, almost as if heaven's angels were shedding tears, too, and we were all forced to leave. I'm sorry more people couldn't have stayed a while with Silas and Ethyl, but only the Fredricksons did. I saw Clara safely home, then spent the next few days snowbound.

In Liberty, Minta had been spending the nights in a bedroll on Frank and Lulabelle's kitchen floor, since her parents had the spare bedroom at Posts'. She wanted to make coffee when she got up but didn't want to wake anyone. As she sat on the floor, hugging her knees and watching the sun rise through the east window, Lulabelle came into the kitchen rubbing her back.

"I am ready for this baby to come out!" Lulabelle said. She looked down at her stomach and yelled, "Did you hear that?"

Minta laughed. "Stop. You'll wake Frank."

"I don't care. This is all his fault."

"Good. I'm glad you finally feel that way."

"Oh, I hope so. I'm still a little afraid. I just want it to be over so I'll know."

"You may not know. You may not be able to tell for sure. Lots of babies don't look like either of their parents, or anyone else in their families. That's why God makes them so lovable, so you'll love them no matter what they look like."

Lulabelle frowned and stomped her foot. "Don't tell me what I will or won't do. You're not *my* teacher."

"My, you're cranky this morning. Let's change the subject."

"All right. Sorry. I didn't sleep hardly at all last night. I felt really out of sorts, as Grandmother would say. When *your* mother comes, we're going to make you a birthday cake. I wanted ch . . . ch . . . the brown kind, but she reminded me you always want angel food on your birthday."

"This will be my first cake, and celebration, since I left home. Edmund said it was sinful to celebrate birthdays because it meant you were self-centered."

"Don't mention that name in my house, Minta."

"I'm sorry. I won't again."

"Now what are you apologizing for?" Frank said as he came into the room yawning. "You people sure do get up early."

"I couldn't sleep, thanks to you," Lulabelle said.

"Ha. That's nothing compared to the sleep you'll lose once *he* gets here and wants to eat all day and all night." Frank tried to pat her stomach as she turned away from him.

"It's not fair that fathers can't nurse their children. You should have to lose sleep, too."

"I'm sure I'll lose my share. You'll see to that even if he doesn't." He sighed. "It seems not too long ago we were losing sleep for a much pleasanter reason."

"Frank! Don't talk that way in front of Minta!"

"Why not? I'm sure she knows . . ."

Lulabelle turned pale and sat down suddenly in a kitchen chair.

"What's the matter, sweetheart? Are you feeling all right?" Frank ran to her side.

"I feel . . . something. Oh!" Her eyes widened. "Get a towel, Minta. I think my water just broke. I was having stomach cramps all night, but I thought it was just something I ate. Maybe it wasn't. It's early for the baby to . . . oh!" A contraction turned her look of joy into a grimace.

"Go for the doctor, Frank," Minta said, "and my mother. I'll see to Lulabelle until you get back."

After Frank left, Minta helped Lulabelle change into a fresh nightgown and lie down on the bed. She cleaned up the kitchen chair and floor and ran back and forth checking on Lulabelle who had decided she was, in fact, in pain. It was a relief when her mother came in, and a few minutes later, the doctor. Her father and Matthew took Frank down to the store to calm him and wait for developments. Minta wished she could leave, too. She'd never seen a human birth before, but knew she had to be here for this one. Her father hadn't even let her watch the farm animals give birth. He said it wasn't something a young girl should see.

She lost track of the time as she followed the doctor's instructions for boiling water and clean cloths and tried not to focus on Lulabelle's cries of pain. It seemed to take a very long time, but when it was over, the doctor said, "That was easy. Of course, the baby's pretty small—might be a little premature. She was lucky for a first one to come so quickly and easily."

It hadn't looked or sounded at all easy to Minta. She hoped she'd never see one that wasn't easy. She remembered when baby Jaime Archuleta was born last year, and little Teresa had told her about all the blood. Maria had almost died, and Jaime, too, but Minta hadn't been on the scene until after it was all over. She took care of the Archuleta girls until Archie brought his wife back from the hospital, and Alice Fredrickson had wet-nursed Jaime along with her own newborn, James. Praise God, both mother and baby had lived.

Lulabelle was lying with her eyes closed while Minta's mother held the newly cleaned-up little boy—the little boy with a mass of dark hair. Lulabelle had taken one look at him and closed her eyes. Minta saw the tears that slipped out from under the closed lids. Minta took the doctor aside. "Would you tell her that babies are often born with dark hair, and then it turns light later? She might be upset that the baby doesn't look like her, or Frank."

Lulabelle opened her eyes when the doctor explained about the hair. He told her babies were all born with blue eyes, too, but sometimes they turned brown later. Lulabelle looked up in alarm. "His eyes can't turn brown! Frank and I both have blue. I can't have a brown-eyed baby!"

"I didn't say they would, just that they *could*. If you have any brown eyes in your family, they might. Brown seems to be dominant in eyes as well as hair. Why does it matter? He's a handsome little feller, and I expect he'll stay that way no matter what color his eyes and hair are."

Lulabelle didn't answer. All Minta could think of were Edmund's brown eyes—so dark they often looked black.

The baby started to cry, and Minta's mother, who had cleaned and wrapped him, lay him in the crook of Lulabelle's arm. "See if he'll take some milk," she said. "Sometimes they don't right away. Land sakes, it's been a long time since I held a baby. But I remember everything."

"No. It's too soon," Lulabelle said. "Don't . . ." Minta's mother unbuttoned the front of Lulabelle's nightgown and guided the small head to a nipple where it nuzzled a minute, like a kitten searching its mother's belly, and then latched on. As Lulabelle felt the suction, she turned to look fully at the baby for the first time. His lips lost their hold, and she gently guided herself back into his mouth.

"That's right," the doctor said, "he's getting the idea. You both are. Is anyone going to go get the father? I'm ready for my cigar."

"Of course," Minta said. "I'll go tell him."

"Just him!" Lulabelle called. "I don't want all those other men in here!"

At least Lulabelle was sounding more like herself.

So Minta spent another birthday without cake or celebration. Everyone, even her own mother, seemed to forget it was her birthday, too. But she didn't mind. Her birthday had never been celebrated much since it came so close on the heels of Christmas. She was just relieved that Frank Junior was here and healthy. When her mother finally let her hold the baby, she peered into the little face. She couldn't see anything of Frank there, or of Edmund, for that matter. The still blue eyes looked a little like Lulabelle's. "You're just your own self, aren't you,

Frankie?" she whispered. "And I was right. I love you, and everyone else will, too."

A few days later, Minta's mother came to her senses long enough to remember she had once given birth, too. She made the delayed angel food cake and gave Minta the skirt she had sewn for her out of a soft, gray flannel. Now Minta could wear her old, black church skirt for school and this new one for church. Lulabelle had made her two gingham aprons, and Frank let her pick out a bolt of fabric to make the curtains she'd been wanting for the school. Her father self-consciously handed her two tortoiseshell combs for her hair. "I like how you're wearing your hair up now, darling," he said. "It suits you. Twenty-one in 1921—my New Century Gal is all grown up. Just like the century and this country. It's fitting we spent your birthday in a place called Liberty."

CHAPTER THIRTEEN

Travel Plans

✦

Devil's Creek Missouri, January 1921

Sari watched Eddie looking at himself in the mirror. He seemed to admire his crooked nose and gray hair. He always smiled when he talked about his new looks. More and more she was finding out what a strange man he was. The winter kept him cooped up with her in the house more, and his bad temper was even worse. She was beginning to wonder if it wouldn't have been better if she and Orville had just left him down by the creek to die.

He was in a good mood today, though. He'd been down to the creek earlier and come back chuckling to himself. Ever since then he kept going to the mirror and looking at himself.

"What's got you so all-fired-up today?" she asked. "What'd you see down at the crick?"

He turned and smiled at her in that wicked way he had. If he had a handlebar mustache, which he didn't, she imagined he'd twist it while he smiled. "Met some men down there," he said.

"What was they doin'?"

"Looking for bones. The creek's pretty low right now what with the drought and all, so they was looking for bones."

"Yeah. A lot of people have died in that crick, and most of their bodies was never found. Was they lookin' for anyone in particular?"

"Some wanted man they think fell in last year."

"Oh, yeah. I heard about that—a few weeks after you come to us. Of course you was pretty bad off then. You probly don't remember none of it. Orville went to town and seen the wanted poster. Looked real mean, Orville said. Some murderer from Iowa, or maybe Indiana, as I recall. A lot younger than you, though."

"Yeah, I saw. They showed me pictures of him." He laughed and looked in the mirror again. "I told them I hadn't seen anyone like that around here. They asked if I knew you. Said they didn't want to come up to the house 'cause last time they did you gave them a shower of buckshot for their trouble."

"I don't cotton to no strangers coming to my door."

"You let me in."

"That was different. You was half-dead. I wasn't worried about you giving me any trouble. You don't 'spose that wanted man's still 'round hereabouts, do you? I noticed the other day we're missing some stuff from the barn."

"Naw. He probably drowned in the creek like they think he did. I told them they was wasting their time around here and they believed me. Went on downstream."

It was the longest conversation they'd had in ages. Usually she could only get one word answers and grunts out of Eddie. Unless he was mad at her for something, and then he'd let loose a whole string of words, followed by blows. She guessed she knew why Orville left. Mostly Eddie got mad when he counted the egg money, which was at least once a day—like it might have magically changed overnight. Whatever he wanted it for, it wasn't enough. And he seemed to think it was her fault the chickens weren't laying more eggs or that the grocer in town wasn't paying more for them. She'd noticed that nothing ever was Eddie's fault.

As if he could read her mind, he turned to her and said, "We've got to get more money by spring. I was thinking we can butcher the pigs and chickens and sell them. And we'll sell the cow, too, right before we go."

"Go? Eddie, I know *you're* planning a trip. But I'm not going nowhere, and I need the animals to live on here."

"Of course you're going with me. We have to go as man and wife."

"We're getting married, finally? Oh, Eddie . . ."

"No, you idiot. I said we have to go 'as man and wife,' so people think we are. You know I can't marry yet. That's why we're going, remember? So's I can fix it so I can."

"But . . ."

"Shut up your arguing! I told you how it's going to be. That's all you need to know."

Sari wanted to ask, "What if Orville comes back and finds us gone?" But once Eddie said "shut up," it was a good idea to shut up. Dare she hope he really was going to fix it so's they could get hitched? Then she'd have a man to help around the place and maybe she could have more kids. Eddie wanted kids, too. He said a man needed lots of sons to help him farm. Too bad he drove Orville away. Orville could've learned to help the way Eddie wanted. She wondered where Orville had gone. He'd always talked about going out west, like life would be better out there. She didn't know where he got that fool idea. Life was probably harder out there—especially for a boy alone. She wished she had Orville back. Then she wouldn't need Eddie so much.

And *how* was Eddie gonna fix it so's they could get married if he already was? He must be planning on going to ask his wife for a divorce. That would be why he had to go on this trip. She wasn't sure she wanted to go wherever it was Eddie was going, but if it meant a chance to get married again, she would. She didn't want to spend the rest of her life alone. Besides, she had brought Eddie into her house, and now she didn't know how to get him out of it. Best just to leave things as they was and see what worked out. If only she still had Orville here to help. Two of them, plus surprise, plus a gun, might be able to get rid of Eddie, if necessary. She'd be a fool to try it alone.

Chapter Fourteen

Softball Roster

❧❦❧

Thursday, February 17, 1921, Rockytop—*It seems winter is over. We had a few snow storms, but since February began, it's been unseasonably warm and dry. "False spring," Fred calls it. The kids are getting a lot of softball practice in. They are anxious to get their final positions on the team set, so they can start practicing for the tournament in earnest. To that end, I have invited Silas, Richard, and Ernst to come today and act as a panel of judges to decide who's best suited for which position. If I decide, I will surely make someone mad, as both Michael and Solly want to be the pitcher. If I let the kids decide, they'd probably come to blows before they got it sorted out. The sooner it's decided, the better. They don't seem to be able to concentrate on schoolwork when they have these "more important" matters on their minds.*

I talked to the men about judging on Sunday after Meg's christening. Seems the whole valley was there. Well, except the Stonacres, of course. I stood next to Claudia while Silas stood next to Fred, so my fears about standing up in church with Silas proved to be silly as I should have known they were. No one seemed to think anything about two unmarried people being the godparents. I do feel a special bond with Meg now as I hope Silas does. It's wonderful to live in a place where neighbors take care of each other, even to the point of taking responsibility for each others' children. Of course, as the teacher, I do that anyway.

Minta had to stop writing to let Blackie in. The cat had learned to jump up on a window sill and rake her claws down the glass, making a bone-chilling sound like chalk squeaking on a blackboard, a sound that couldn't be ignored for long. Blackie had decided she was a two-household cat after having spent the summer with Valoris. They kept trying to return her to Minta, but Blackie had other ideas. She split her time between the two places now, usually spending the nights with Minta, since Minta allowed her on the bed. When Minta rang the first bell for school, Blackie disappeared, knowing the noisy children were on the way. She'd had enough of being packed around like a doll-baby last year. She also knew what time Paulo milked the cow, and always managed to be in the barn then, standing on her hind legs as he squirted liquid into her mouth. Paul and Gina had invited Minta over one day especially to see that event.

The students' excitement was hard to contain until afternoon recess when the three judges were to arrive. Minta breathed a sigh of relief when she heard them coming, and she dismissed everyone for recess a few minutes early.

Silas organized the children into groups, and the three men watched them throw, pitch, catch, and hit. Minta was pleased to see they gave equal time to each child on each skill, even the younger ones who had no realistic chance of being the pitcher or catcher. That meant they weren't finished by the time recess was over, so she allowed them to continue until they were done.

"All right, children, time to go in," she called. "The judges need time to meet and decide."

"But we want to know!" Robert said.

"I'm sure you do," Minta replied, "but that's not going to happen yet. Inside, now!"

After the children were inside, Minta turned to the three men. "How do you want to do this?"

"I brought paper and pen," Ernst said. "We'll decide, make a list, and give it to you after school. Then tomorrow morning you can tell them what we decided."

"So I get to be the bad guy, and you'll be long gone when all the wailing and whining starts," Minta said.

"Yeah, that's kind of what we planned," Richard said sheepishly.

"Isn't that what you get paid for, Minta?" Silas asked with a smile. "To handle the wailing and whining."

"I guess. But I'm usually the one who causes it."

If Minta thought it was hard to contain the children before, it was nearly impossible after recess. She had to make a rule that no one could get up and look out the window at the three judges leaning on the fence as they discussed their options. She threatened to keep everyone after school if they didn't apply themselves to their lessons. She broke up several whispered conversations speculating about which judge seemed to like whom better and who might get what position.

"It's not fair," Robert said when she told him again to quit talking about it and get to work. "There's all these new kids this year, but those of us who had our positions last year should get first choice of getting the same position back."

"Don't you want Rockytop to win this year?" Minta asked. "The judges will pick the ones they think give us the best chance of doing that."

"No, they won't," Solly said. "Since Michael's brother's a judge, he'll probably get pitcher even though I'm better."

"No, you're not," Robert defended his brother while Michael glowered.

"I'm sure *all* the judges will be fair," Minta said. "But even if they aren't, there are three of them. Two will overrule one. Now, for the last time, we are *done* discussing this. When the results are posted tomorrow morning, I expect all of you to accept the judges' decision with grace and good nature. And, as of right now, *everyone* has two strikes. The next one who talks out of turn will have three and face punishment."

After school the children formed knots to walk home together— the Haleys in one knot, the Stonacres in another, and the Valoris and Fredricksons in the third. Minta couldn't hear what they were whispering to each other and was just as glad she couldn't. When they'd all disappeared in their various directions, Silas reappeared. Minta was dismayed when she saw that he had stayed behind, and Ernst and Richard were gone. It was getting harder and harder to be alone with Silas.

"Chicken," she said, trying to keep her tone light. "Where were you hiding until they all left?"

"Would you believe I had to use the outhouse?"

"Not really."

"Boy, those kids take this seriously, don't they?"

"You should know that from the tournament last year."

Silas looked across the playing field, a pensive expression on his face. "Last year I could hardly watch the tournament," he said. "I left early. It was just too hard to be there—so close to you. I kept thinking about what we'd talked about and how I'd lost you forever."

"Silas, please, let's not go over all that again. Do you have the list for me?"

"Yes, and something else."

Minta sighed. Why did he have to make everything so complicated? "What now, Silas? Really I can't take . . ."

"It's not what you're thinking. It's a letter. I picked it up yesterday, and I thought you might want someone with you when you read it." He fished it out of his shirt pocket and handed it to her. "See? The post-mark's smudged, but I think it says it's from Missouri. Callaway County." He handed her the envelope.

Minta opened it with shaking fingers. She read quickly and silently.

"What's it say, Minta?" Silas asked. "Is it about *him*?"

"It says they searched the stream for his bones when the water got low like they promised they would. They didn't find any. Well, they found some bones, but they were a small child's—one who had disappeared a few years ago, they think. And they found a broken pair of handcuffs, but there's no way to tell where they were from or how long they'd been there. But they said the handcuffs were consistent with having been on a body that eventually decomposed and broke apart. So *they* think it confirms his death." She crumpled the letter and held it balled in her fist.

"I'm sorry, Minta," Silas said. "I was hoping you'd find out something definite."

"Not as much as I was."

"Yes, Minta. I think I am hoping it as much as you. It's my life, my future, too."

"It doesn't have to be. You have the choice to walk away from this situation. I don't."

"You know I've made my choice. I'm with you. Whatever it takes. However long it takes." He took a step toward her.

She turned away. "Oh, Silas, I don't deserve you. What a mess I've made of my life! Of our lives."

She turned and started walking back toward the school, the sharp edges of the paper ball poking into the soft flesh of her palm like a prickly reminder of Edmund.

"Minta," Silas called, "don't you want this softball list?"

She turned. "Not really. But I suppose I have to take it, too. Thank you for your work today, Silas. And please thank Richard and Ernst for me. I know there were some hard decisions to make."

"Not so hard. We just went with the ones who showed us they could do the jobs. You tell them that tomorrow. Tell them *all* the judges agreed on *all* the positions. And tell them we expect them to play their best at the tournament and make us proud of Rockytop. You can bet we'll all be there cheering them on."

"I'll tell them, Silas. And it would help if you all told them when you see them, too. They put a lot of stock in what you young men think. That's why I asked you three to judge instead of the school board members."

After Silas left, Minta allowed herself a rare cry. She wasn't sure if she was crying over Silas or over the hard day ahead of her tomorrow. Both, probably. She felt better after she splashed her face with water from the bucket. Then she read the list Silas had given her and felt worse.

The next morning Minta posted the list on the front blackboard. Fridays were often difficult, and she suspected this one would be even more so. Above the list, she wrote:

EVERYONE WHO PLAYS WELL IS A WINNER.
ROCKYTOP SOFTBALL TEAM, 1921
CATCHER/COACH—ANGUS
PITCHER—SOLLY
RELIEF PITCHER/SECOND BASE—MICHAEL
FIRST BASE—CLARA
THIRD BASE—GUNNY
SHORTSTOP—ROBERT
RIGHT FIELD—MARY
CENTER FIELD—PAUL
LEFT FIELD—GERTIE
OUTFIELDERS: ELEANOR, JUDY, EVERETT, DALE,
DENNIS, BETH, GINA

Minta stood in front of the list until morning exercises were over and all the students were seated. "When I move aside," she said, "you may *quietly* read the list. At recess we will start practicing with these positions. I will *not* tolerate any discussion, questions, comments, or complaints about this list until recess. *Is that clear?*" When they'd all nodded solemnly, she moved aside.

There were a few gasps and disgusted snorts, but nothing she could classify as any of the things she had forbidden. Solly's eyes widened in disbelief, but he contained himself and didn't jump up in triumph as she'd been afraid he would. She would have to remember to compliment him on his self-control later. She snuck a peek at Michael out of the corner of her eye, but his face was stone-like and unreadable, his arms held rigidly at his sides.

"All right then," she said. "Your assignments are on the side board as usual. I want the first and second graders on the recitation bench with your readers. The rest of you begin your lessons."

She had planned individual assignments for today instead of the usual group work. The less chance they had to whisper together, the less likely they'd work themselves up into a snit before recess. As she listened to the little ones read, she kept a wary eye on the others, but they all seemed to be bent to their tasks. For once she didn't look forward to recess. She wished the morning could continue as quietly and orderly as it seemed to be starting.

Before letting the students out for recess, Minta called them to attention. "Silas asked me to tell you that all the judges agreed on all the positions. And he said they're counting on each one of you to play your very best and to make them proud of the Rockytop Rattlers. Remember, it's not whether we win or lose, it's . . ."

"How we play the game," several of them dutifully recited.

Eleanor raised her hand.

"Yes, Eleanor?"

"Can, I mean, may, I ask a question now, or am I gonna get in trouble for asking if I can ask a question?"

"You may ask a question."

"What if I don't want to play softball? It's dumb. I'd rather sit with you on the sidelines and yell for our team."

"The rules for the tournament are that every student in the school has to play on the team. That's why we have so many outfielders."

"That's good," Gertie said. "It means someone will be close to almost any fair ball to catch it."

"You're a good runner, Eleanor. We need you on the team," Angus said, and Minta silently blessed him.

"What good are a bunch of outfielders if they can't catch?" Robert said, looking at Gina and Beth. "And why can't *I* be first base like last year? We can't have a *girl* in the infield. Are you sure they didn't make a mistake when they put Clara on first?"

"Where were you during the trials, Robert?" Angus asked. "Clara's good at catching, she's left-handed which is a plus on first, and she's a lot taller than you. She can catch the high balls you might miss."

"But she's a *girl*," Robert insisted.

"So?" Gertie said. "I'm a girl, and I'll bet I could take you down. I can take Gunny down, some of the time, at least. Want me to prove it at recess?"

Minta stepped in. "No one's going to take anyone down. We're just going to play softball. Are there any other problems we need to address before we start?" She looked pointedly at Michael who hadn't stopped frowning since she announced it was time for recess. He sat back in his seat, his arms folded.

"What's a relief pitcher?" Paul asked. "And how come Michael gets to do two things?"

"A relief pitcher is in case the regular pitcher needs to be replaced—like if he gets sick or tired or even just isn't playing well. If that happens, Michael will pitch and Robert will move to second base and Mary will move to short stop," Minta answered.

"Who decides? You?" Solly asked.

"No. That would be the coach. Angus will decide if you need to be replaced."

"Oh, good. He's a Haley. I can see how that's going to go. I might as well be too tired right now."

"Come on, Solly," Angus said. "I won't replace you unless I really need to. I want the best players playing."

"Thanks a lot!" Michael finally broke his silence. "I pitched last year and we almost won."

"Yeah, *almost*," Gertie said. "You pitched that home run that won the game for Halpern."

Several argumentative voices were raised with accusations flying back and forth.

Minta picked up a book and dropped it on the desk with a loud slap. "That's enough!" she said in the startled silence. "Now, you have two choices. Choice one is you go out and practice softball with grace and good nature as I said yesterday. Choice two is you sit in here and compose a letter to the school board and the superintendent about why you are withdrawing from the tournament this year. Which is it going to be?"

They played softball. They weren't all happy about it. Grace and good nature were still a ways away, but a semblance of harmony was achieved.

CHAPTER FIFTEEN

Fire and Friendship

✌ ❦ ❧

Monday, March 21, 1921, Rockytop—*March has been a cruel month. The false spring of February is over and we have cold wind most days. I'm using the wood stove almost as much as in the dead of winter. It freezes every night leaving a crust of ice along the edges of the creek. There has been little moisture to go with the wind, so we often have dust devils swirling through the schoolyard. Just the other day I had to wash out eyes and pick twigs out of hair after one went through softball practice. The kids have even lost their enthusiasm for practice. It's hard to focus on your goals when a cold wind is blowing your hair into your eyes and the dust is choking you.*

On a happier note, Angus is making real progress toward the Eighth Grade Exam. Mary has finished most of the sixth grade work and will be moving to seventh soon. Solly has almost caught up with the other seventh graders in all subjects but math. Clara is still an indifferent student, more interested in gossip than in school work. She has really matured physically this year, into a woman, and has started to pay more atten-tion to personal hygiene. At least none of the boys are interested in her that way. I'm not looking forward to Mary's maturing. The only boy old enough for her who is not her relative is Solly, and I can't imagine the two of them together. It could be a match as bad as Edmund's and mine.

Michael is still causing as many problems as he can without bringing down the wrath of his father. I hadn't realized he was such a manipulator. He tells his parents one thing at home and me something completely different at school. I suppose some day he may be able to put those skills to good use, but I fail to see how.

Minta went to sleep thinking about the challenges her various students presented, especially Michael and Solly. She had found that often when she went to sleep thinking about a problem, the solution would come to her the next day.

She was dreaming. Dennis was ringing the bell, and all the children were yelling, "Wolf, wolf! A big, bad wolf is going to get you, Miss Mayfield." She twisted and turned over in bed, tangling the covers around her and upsetting Blackie who jumped to the floor. As she opened her eyes, the sound of the bell still rang in her ears.

Then she jerked herself fully awake. The bell *was* ringing! With some difficulty, she untangled herself from the quilt and threw it around her shoulders. She hurried through the school room to the front door and opened it.

Instead of Dennis, she found Ernst ringing the bell. He stopped when he saw her.

"What is it, Ernst? What's wrong?" she asked.

He turned and pointed south. Her eyes found the red glow that could only be flames. "I was doing the nightly patrol and saw the flames," he said. "I'm going to ride over there now. You stay here and tell people who come what's going on. But probably most of them will see the flames and head that way instead."

"Is that trees burning? And where is it? I can't tell how far away it is."

"No, it's not trees. There aren't any right there. It's got to be a building—on either Silas' or the Stonacres' place. I've got to hurry. I hope it's not one of the houses, but that's the most likely this time of night." He ran to his horse which was waiting by the well trough.

"Wait!" Minta called. "I want to go with you! I can help with the children if it's at the Stonacres'."

"The Haleys will have to come by here," he called over his shoulder as he rode off. "Get a ride with them."

Minta ran back into her bedroom and threw on her gingham work dress and boots. She put on her coat and scarf as she was going back outside. The flames were brighter now, the red glow pulsating like a living being. Something was fueling the fire. She didn't want to think about what it might be. While she waited, she did the only thing she could: pray. She found herself praying that it would not be Silas' house, and that he and his mother were all right.

Finally she saw Fred riding down the road and ran out to meet him. He'd already seen the flames and wasn't going to stop at the school. No one else had come, either. That meant they'd already headed in the right direction.

"Fred! Take me with you!" Minta called.

"Wait for Claudia. She's bringing the wagon with some supplies we might need. You can help her with the children."

Minta stood shivering by the road until the wagon appeared, white mist rising from the horses' nostrils. She hopped up next to Claudia. Several children were in the back with buckets, shovels, ropes, and a basket of what was probably food. "Jump out and get the school buckets, Angus," Claudia said.

"Where's Meg?" Minta asked, looking around for the baby.

"I left the younger kids with Rachel. Just brought the ones big enough to be of help. I've started giving Meg cow's milk once in a while, so Rachel should be able to make do."

After Angus returned with the buckets, they didn't try to talk any more over the noise of the wagon and its contents bouncing along the rutted road. Claudia drove too fast, but no one complained, just gritted their teeth and held on. The red glow drew them along like moths to a candle flame, and smoke began to sting their eyes. Real flames were visible now, reaching up into the night sky.

"It's close," Claudia shouted. "It must be at the Stonacres'."

It was. The barn was fully engulfed in flames, and men were running back and forth from the well with buckets and water. Claudia passed out the buckets she'd brought to the oldest kids and told Minta to take the younger ones who were running around the yard to a safe spot and keep them there. The Stonacre kids were still in their nightclothes, shivering and staring with wide eyes at the barn. "Let's go inside and get you some warmer clothes," Minta said. "Then we'll come back outside." She knew if an ember from the barn blew onto the house roof it could go up, too. She didn't want to be inside if that happened.

Finally she had all the Stonacre children, except Solly and Clara who were helping with buckets, corralled in a corner of the yard with the Fredrickson twins. She noticed Sophie Valori and her children weren't there. Of course, Sophie couldn't very well leave little Joseph, who had seizure problems, alone or bring him to something like this. Alice Fredrickson and her two little ones weren't there either or Sally Mae who was almost nine months along. It appeared everyone else was, including Silas and his mother who was using a broom and her feet to beat out flames that started in the dry grasses.

"Miss Mayfield, we want to help!" Eleanor said.

"Yeah!" Gunny and Gertie said together.

"The best help you can be is to stay out of the way," Minta said. The disappointment on their faces made her reconsider. "See what Silas' mother is doing?" she asked. "Do you all have on good, heavy boots? Then you can help her by stomping out little embers that fall on the ground so they don't start fires in the grass. The wind is blowing them this way. Try to watch where they fall and then run and stomp them out. I'll do it, too," she said. She picked up Charlie and balanced him on one hip and put Gracie on the other.

As the children scattered, she yelled, "Two rules! Stay where I can see you, and stay away from the barn."

The children looked like they were doing a dance with the devil in hell. They ran from spot to spot stomping and jumping up and down. The roar of the fire behind them sounded like a mountain waterfall in flood season. Minta found it was all she could do to keep an eye on the children and hold on to Charlie and Gracie. The wind had been blowing the smoke away from them, but now they were running into it after the fallen embers. Her eyes stung and watered. Charlie and then Gracie began to cry.

She turned and looked back at the barn. There would be no saving it. All the efforts being expended were simply to keep the fire from spreading. Buckets were being passed down the line from person to person. Near the end of the line, Michael swung a bucket to Solly who passed it on to Silas who threw the water on the flames. Then he threw the empty bucket to Clara or Mary who ran it back to the well where Fred was filling them as fast as he could. As Minta turned to watch the children, something caught the corner of her eye. She turned back and focused on the house. There was a glow on the porch roof. It had caught fire! She handed the two little ones to Eleanor and Gertie. Then she ran to the bucket brigade that was strung out from the well to the barn.

"The house!" she screamed. "The roof's on fire."

The bucket brigade shifted directions, and everyone hurried to put out the fire on the porch roof. Solly and Michael came running with a ladder and set it up against the house. Richard climbed up to dump the water onto the roof. Michael and Solly seemed to be working as one unit, not even needing to talk to each other, just pitching in and helping, working as hard as Angus and the men. Minta wished she could see that kind of cooperation between them at school.

Thanks to everyone's quick actions, the house was saved, with only the porch damaged beyond repair. As the sun came up in the east, everyone sat or lay down wherever they could find an unburned grassy spot to take a much-needed break. The exhaustion showed on the black-streaked faces. There was still a lot to do, putting out hot spots and making sure nothing rekindled. Minta and the children carried buckets of water and drinking cups among the tired people, offering them drinks. She noticed that Claudia, Hannah, and Mrs. Stonacre had disappeared. She asked Fred where they were, and he said they'd gone down to Hannah's to prepare something to eat for everyone. They were all going to go down there for breakfast to get away from the smoke. They'd eat in two shifts, so one group could make sure everything was kept under control while the other ate.

Minta walked all the children down the road to the Fredricksons' with the first group. Now that all the excitement was over, they were tired and hungry. Charlie was crying for his mother, while Gracie was fussy, needed to be changed, and had a runny nose. Even Clara couldn't settle them down. Minta was relieved to reunite all the children with their mothers, so she didn't have total responsibility for them.

After Minta helped Claudia serve everyone the hastily prepared biscuits, gravy, and eggs, they sat on the porch step to rest. "What a night!" Claudia said, running her fingers through her tangled hair.

"Well, it could have turned out a lot worse," Minta said. "I'm so thankful no one was injured."

"That's true, but the Stonacres still lost a lot. They got some of the animals out, but not all of them. And the barn itself is a big loss. We'll have to help them rebuild—the barn as well as the porch. Poor Ruby is beside herself. She doesn't handle stress well."

"Ruby?" Minta asked.

"Ruby. Mrs. Stonacre."

"Oh. I guess I never knew her first name. She wouldn't tell me when I went over there. So you're on a first name basis now?"

"Have been for quite a while. I told you we were visiting regularly."

"Has she told you anything . . . you know . . . about how Sol treats her? Or have you seen any evidence of . . ."

"No, Minta. She seems to love Sol. She defends him."

"I can't believe that! I didn't love Edmund, and I certainly would never have defended him, if anyone asked, which no one did."

"I think you've been trying to see too much of Edmund in Sol. No one is all black or all white. Edmund was mostly black, but Sol has a lot of gray in him, if that makes any sense. Ruby just says Sol has always had a hard time handling anger but that he's getting a little calmer as he gets older. Sometimes the kids just push him too far. I'm sure you know how they can be."

"Yes, I do," Minta said. But she thought of Michael instead of the Stonacre kids. There had been times this year when she had almost lashed out at Michael in inappropriate ways. It was easy to see how it might happen. But that meant adults had to be even more careful how they handled anger. Minta turned and looked across the valley at the undamaged cabins visible along the road. She realized she was judging people and applying her own standards to them. Probably everyone did that to some extent, but that didn't make it right. She had the advantage of being able to send the children home every day. She was just responsible for their learning at school, not all the things their parents had to teach them and prepare them for. She was beginning to see that being a parent was an even tougher job than being a teacher.

Minta turned back to Claudia. "I'm just surprised Ruby, I don't know, opened up to you, I guess."

"Well, we've got a lot in common, Minta. Her eight kids are similar ages to my seven. There's always a lot for mothers to talk to each other about."

"I've tried to talk to her."

"I know you have. But, no offense, Minta, you can be intimidating, especially to someone like Ruby who isn't very well educated. You're the teacher, after all."

"I don't mean to be intimidating!"

"I know you don't. You can't help how you look and talk. And we want our teacher to be well educated. You just need to know that some people aren't comfortable with you."

"I guess I do know that," Minta admitted. She thought of all the times adults had come into the school for some reason and acted awkward, like they felt out of place—Silas, Luke Woods, even the sheriff. She guessed it was just part of her job. She had to maintain her image as the teacher, even if it made some people uncomfortable. But that made *her* uncomfortable. She wanted to fit in—to be just like the other valley residents. She was still partly an outsider in spite of all the experiences she shared with the others. She thought of Claudia as her best friend but, of course, Claudia and Ruby really had a lot more in common and were closer to the same age.

After breakfast everyone gathered back at the Stonacres to decide what to do next. It was a solemn group that stood around the barn, looking at the smoldering remains.

"I wonder what started it?" Silas said. "We haven't had any lightning lately."

Sol looked at Solly and asked, "You did take that lantern I was using in the horse stall into the house when I told you to, didn't you?"

Solly looked up, his eyes confused for a minute, frowning as he tried to remember. Then his face went white and he took a step back.

"You didn't! Damn it, boy . . ." Sol started toward his son.

Fred stepped between them. "Hold on, now, Sol," he said. "There's probably no way to tell what started it for sure. Things happen. That's part of living out here the way we do. What's done is done. Let's look at how we can make things right from here on out."

Suddenly ill at ease, people started moving away, back toward the house. Minta went with them. She looked back. Sol, Fred, and Solly still stood in the same positions. Silas walked over to them and said something to Sol. Then the three men walked off together leaving Solly standing alone, his arms dangling from bent, dejected shoulders, his head bowed. Michael and Angus approached Solly and spoke to him. Then the three of them walked off as the men had.

It was agreed there would be no school on this day after the fire. Everyone was too tired. Minta said a silent prayer that Solly would come to school the next day and that he'd be all right. Her prayer that the fire not be at Silas' had been answered, but at the expense of the Stonacres. She felt guilty about that. She hadn't even thought about praying for the Stonacres. Was it possible that a prayer for something good for one person would cause something bad to happen to someone else? Their lives were getting all tangled up in spite of Sol's attempt to keep his family isolated. Ruby and Claudia. Michael and Solly. Eleanor and Gertie. Even Minta and Silas—their lives were tangled up, too. Sometimes she wasn't sure what she should pray for. She had stopped short of praying for Edmund's death—well, if *wishing* were different from praying. She wasn't sure they weren't the same thing, but surely it was a sin to pray for another human being to die. Unless they were really old and ready to die. Her grandmother had prayed to die at the end and asked others to pray for her death. Minta hadn't been able to say that prayer, either.

She was tired and confused. She resolved she would pray only for good things from now on. She had to have faith that her latest prayer for Solly would be answered.

Chapter Sixteen

Work To Do

Monday, April 11, 1921, Rockytop—*What a weekend! I never worked so hard or had so much fun. We all met at the Stonacres' to start the rebuilding. We were going to do it last weekend, but little Richard Frederick (Dick) Haley decided to make his entrance, and everyone was helping at Richard and Sally Mae's instead. It's funny to think little Dick and his aunt Meg will be in the same grade in school some day.*

At Claudia's suggestion, instead of replacing the Stonacres' porch, a new bedroom is being added. Now there will be more room for all the children. The frame and roof of the barn was completed this weekend. Of course, there's still a lot of work for Sol and Solly to do, but all the jobs that take more than two men got done. The children who were too young to help in other ways cleaned up after the men, picking up dropped nails, scrap wood, and so forth.

No one worked harder than Solly. I hope his father can see he doesn't need to punish him. He's punishing himself. He wouldn't even stop working to come up to the house to eat lunch, so Clara took him some food. He's been very subdued ever since the fire. When he first came back to school, I looked for evidence of a beating but didn't see anything obvious.

We had a huge potluck for lunch. After lunch the women made soap. This was also Claudia's suggestion. There were all the ashes from the barn, and she and Ruby leached the lye water from them ahead, and the rest of us brought all the bacon drippings and tallow we had been saving. We simmered it all for several hours and then scented some of it with dried rose petals the Haley girls had saved from the wild roses last summer and some of it with dried mint. So everyone went home with several balls of soap, which we needed after working in and around the burned-out barn.

My grandmother used to say, "Thank God every day that you have work to do and the strength to do it." I'm beginning to understand what she meant. Work is a blessing. As is health.

The whole school was again working on poetry lessons. This time, Minta had them read poems at their individual reading levels, and each pupil had to memorize one poem to say aloud to the class. The younger students' poems had to be at least four lines long and the older ones at least ten. Then each student had to write a poem. Minta realized she'd made a mistake when she'd made the boys write poems as punishment. It had taken her several weeks of reading a variety of poems to them and making up silly ones herself to convince them that writing poems could be fun. Finally most of the students seemed to be convinced and were at least attempting to write theirs. Those had to be at least four lines long and some of the lines had to rhyme. There was much discussion about whether "blue" rhymed with "through." They decided "almost rhymes" would count, too.

Robert was the first to complete his poem and offer to recite it.

> *Miss Mayfield is our teacher.*
> *She should have been a preacher.*
> *She reads her Bible every day*
> *And teaches the Golden Rule.*
> *But don't get Three Strikes,*
> *Or she'll get out her ferule.*

"You can't rhyme "rule" with "ferule," Gertie said when she quit laughing.

"Why not?" Robert asked.

"It's like rhyming 'school' with 'school'. That doesn't make any sense."

"Hey, 'school' rhymes with 'ferule' too. I need to add some lines."

Minta laughed. "Very good Robert. Who wants to go next?" Clara and Mary both raised their hands. "Okay, Mary, go ahead."

"Clara and I wrote one together," Mary said, "but it's as long as two poems. I hope that's okay."

"We'll see. Let's hear it. Can you both say it together?"

"Sure. We sing together, don't we? In fact, we're going to make music to go with this poem because it's going to be our fight song for Rockytop School. I mean, if everyone likes it."

"If it's a fight song, it better have some fighting words in it," Gunny said.

"It does," Mary assured him. "Now be quiet and listen."

> *We are the Rattlers*
> *The Rockytop Rattlers*
> *When you hear us coming, get out of the way.*
> *'Cause we are the Rattlers*
> *The Rockytop Rattlers*
> *And we will have victory today.*
>
> *At softball the Rattlers are the best.*
> *We can beat Halpern and all the rest.*
> *The Rattlers, the Rattlers, yea, yea, yea!*
>
> *We strike fast like a snake.*
> *Our venom is strong.*
> *That sound that you hear*
> *Means we're coming along.*
>
> *'Cause we are the Rattlers*
> *The Rockytop Rattlers*
> *And we will have victory today.*
> *The Rattlers, the Rattlers, yea, yea, yea!*

Most of the rest of the class joined in on the final "yea, yea's" and then broke into spontaneous applause.

"That's so good," Eleanor said. "Would you teach it to us right now?"

"Let's let them set it to music first," Minta said. "Then we'll all learn it as a class. We'll sing it for everyone before the tournament game."

At morning recess, Minta got Mary and Clara started on their music practice. They were supposed to be working on "Amazing Grace," which they were going to sing in church some Sunday. Minta had gotten Reverend MacIntosch to invite them specially. The Stonacres would never come to church on their own, but maybe they would come to bring Clara so she could sing. That was Minta's plan, anyway. She suspected making the soap had been Claudia's plan to get them cleaned up enough not to offend the other parishioners.

Instead of practicing their church song, the girls wanted to work on their original song. Clara had a tune in her head, which Mary was trying to pick out on the piano. Minta showed them how to make a blank sheet of music, so when they figured out which notes they wanted, they could record them on the staff.

When the two girls were working well on their own, she went outside with the other children. The older boys were disgusted that they only got afternoon recess to practice softball as a whole group, but Minta had finally intervened on behalf of the children who didn't want to play softball twenty-three hours a day. "They'll play better for you if you don't drive them so hard," she told Angus and Michael.

"We just want to win," Angus said.

"I know you do. There are more ways than one to win, you know. If you all improve your skills, and have fun, then I'll consider you winners no matter what happens."

"Teacher-talk," Michael muttered to Angus as they walked away. "If those dumb girls would put as much effort into practice as that dumb song . . ." She couldn't hear them any more, which was just as well for her nerves, and the boys' hides.

Solly had stayed behind with Minta. "We really got a lot done on the new barn and your house this weekend," she commented.

"Still a lot to do. I want to quit school and stay home to work on it, but Pa won't let me."

"Good for him. Summer's coming soon. You can work on it full time then."

"I guess." Solly kicked a hole in the dirt with the toe of his shoe.

"How are you doing, Solly?" Minta asked. "Are you all right?"

"What do you mean?"

"Your father didn't . . . do anything to you, did he? After the fire, I mean?"

"No. I think he was going to, but Ma says Fred's been talking to him a lot about what to do when he gets so mad. That's kinda funny since Fred beats his kids, too."

"Well, Fred does use corporal punishment. But I've never seen bruises or welts on his kids. There's a difference between discipline and abuse. Anyway, I'm glad your father is learning different ways to deal with you."

"I don't know. I kinda wish he had beat me up. This is almost worse, knowing it was probably my fault and not getting no punishment. Now, it's like I have to do more to make up for it."

"So, you decided to punish yourself, is that it?"

"Huh?"

"The way you've been acting, wanting to work instead of come to school. I'm worried about you, Solly. I can't remember the last time I saw you smile. Everyone makes mistakes. One mistake doesn't mean you're unworthy. You just need to learn from your mistakes and try not to make the same one twice."

"I know, but some mistakes are a lot bigger than others. I could've killed my whole family if the house caught on fire, too."

"But it didn't, Solly. And I believe we can thank God for that."

Solly moved a rock around with the toe of his boot. Minta wondered if she'd made a mistake mentioning God. Did he even have a concept of a loving God, or was he imagining a fire and brimstone God who would punish him for his mistakes?

"I just don't know what to do to make it all right again," Solly finally said. All you people coming to help was nice, but I still feel like *I've* got to do more. I don't think anyone trusts me to do stuff any more. How can I get people to trust me again?"

"By being trustworthy, Solly. We are known by our actions. If you act like a person who can be trusted, then you will be. Just take every opportunity to show us that you are responsible. Try to do your chores well and on time. Try to do well in school. Help with your younger siblings. I know it sounds like a lot, but I also know you can do it."

"I been reading to Charlie and Gracie like you said."

"I thought so. Your reading has improved. Do they like it?"

"Charlie does. He can even point to some of the words and say what they are like 'cat' and 'bat'."

"That's wonderful, Solly! That will make my job so much easier when Charlie starts school. See? You're already doing something responsible."

"Speaking of responsible, what are those little kids up to?" Solly pointed to the corner of the yard where Dale, Beth, Gina, and Dennis were crouched over something furry that was moving.

Minta hurried over, afraid they had Blackie cornered and were fixing to get scratched.

It wasn't Blackie; it was a squirrel. It made its escape when Minta startled the children by asking, "What are you doing to that poor animal?"

"Now it done got away, Teacher," Dennis said.

"Yeah. We almost got it measured," Dale said.

"Measured? What are you talking about?"

"Old Man Rickerts always told Mother, 'Don't go plantin' yore garden afore the oak brush leaves is the size of a squirrel's ear.' We was tryin' to see if it was time to plant yet," Dale explained.

"Wouldn't it be easier to measure the oak leaves first?" Solly asked.

"We got one right here," Beth said. She held up a miniscule piece of vegetation.

"It's too early to plant a garden," Solly said, "no matter what size the leaves or the squirrel's ears are. It's got too warm too soon this year, but it won't keep it up. We'll have some more freezes before summer."

"Can we plant a garden at school, Miss Mayfield?" Beth asked.

"Who would take care of it all summer?"

"Can't you water it for us? You live here."

"I don't stay here in the summer, Beth. I'll probably be in Liberty."

"Why don't we plant a pretend garden?" Dale asked. The others quickly agreed, and they began staking out their garden and making rows with sticks in the dirt. Minta and Solly left them to their labors.

"Plant me some sweet corn," Solly called over his shoulder to them. "I sure do like sweet corn."

"It's good to see you smile again, Solly," Minta said, even though the smile had been halfhearted and fleeting. But even that was too good to last. Solly slipped back into his depression after recess, going through the motions of studying but not really applying himself. It didn't help that Michael kept impatiently telling him the words he stumbled over as they read aloud from the geography text. She gripped the edge of her desk to keep from going over and smacking Michael. He wasn't really doing anything wrong, but there was just something about his attitude that drove her crazy.

Every time Minta thought she'd solved a problem, she found another one waiting around the next corner—or the same one in new clothes. She was always telling the children that they had to work hard to master their lessons, that learning didn't come easily. Why should she expect teaching to come easily? She wanted to kick her chair like

Dale did when he was having trouble with a lesson and would cry, "Why does this school stuff got to be so dang-blasted hard?"

CHAPTER SEVENTEEN

Traveling Money

❧❦❧

Devil's Creek Missouri, March 1921

"Much as I hate to, I think we need to be callin' the sheriff," Sari said to Eddie when he got back from town. "There's more tools missing, and I couldn't find the separator this morning. Did you move it?"

"You don't need a separator. Just let the cream rise to the top and skim it off by hand. You've only got one cow."

"That's not the point. The point is a lot of stuff's done gone missin'. The sheriff . . ."

"We're not calling the sheriff. The fact is, I've been selling some stuff. The egg money just isn't growing fast enough. It's almost time to be thinking about leaving."

Sari stopped in mid-step and turned toward Eddie. "*You've* been selling *my* stuff?"

"No, I've been selling *our* stuff. I'm doing this for us. So we can get married like you want. I went into town today to take care of some legal business, and I'm . . ."

"What legal business? You finally fixed it so's we can git hitched?"

"How many times do I have to tell you," Eddie exploded, "that can't happen until after our trip! You're as dense as that worthless son of yours. Now get out of my way before I do something that might make it impossible for you to travel."

He left her standing, shaking, in the middle of the room. So, he was the one responsible for all the missing items. And here she'd been thinking that wanted man must be hiding in the woods and coming on their property to steal. Where was Eddie keeping the money? He hadn't added any to the jar in the cellar. He must have his own stash somewheres. And what was this legal business in town? He was too much for her to figure out.

Eddie came back into the room and plopped a set of papers, pen, and ink bottle on the table in front of her. "There you go, Sari, just sign there and we'll be all ready to go. You *can* sign your name, can't you?"

"Yes, I can. But you know I cain't read. I ain't signing nothing what I don't know what it says. Read it to me."

"There's too many legal words. A lot of 'wherefores' and 'hereinafters' and words like that. I'll just explain it to you. You know how you're always fretting about Orville coming back and finding us gone? I fixed it so that, if he does, he'll have legal rights to the place. Even though he's still not of age, he'll be able to conduct business in your name. You want Orville to be able to take care of himself, don't you?"

"You know I do, Eddie." She hesitated. It was an awful thoughtful thing for Eddie to do, even though he was probably just doing it so she'd go along with him on this trip of his.

"And I got you something else in town," Eddie said, pulling a small box from his pocket. "See if this fits." It was a wedding band, thin and cheap-looking, but a wedding band nevertheless. "You know we got to travel as man and wife, so you got to have a ring." He slipped it on her finger. "You're now Mrs. Edward Smith. Sarah Smith. Can you remember that?"

"Is that your real name Eddie? Smith?"

"No! Yes. Oh, what does it matter? All you need to know is we're Mr. and Mrs. Edward Smith, and we're going to Colorado to look for land to farm, if anyone asks. But most of the time I expect you to keep your mouth shut. It will be a lot healthier for you."

Colorado! He had finally told her where they were going. "Look for land? We don't have enough money . . ."

"Not *really*, Sari! We're going to *pretend* we're looking for land. So we can . . . Oh what's the use of trying to explain anything to you? Just sign the paper." He thrust the pen toward her and took hold of her shoulder with one hand, forcing her down into the chair at the table.

"Is this really for Orville?"

"Yes. See? There's two copies. We'll file one at the courthouse and leave one right here on the table for him to find when he comes back. *He* can read, can't he?"

"Yep. He went all the way through sixth grade. He can read and write real good."

"Okay, then. He'll find the papers, read them, and know he can live here and do what he needs to do until we get back. If we come back. If not, then he . . ."

"Where else would we go, Eddie? You said we're not really going to buy land in Colorado."

"Oh, I don't know. Depends on what happens there. We might want to keep going west. I hear California's a nice place to settle down. Warm there all year. You'd like to see the ocean wouldn't you?"

"I don't know." Sari looked down at the paper. It was all so confusing. Eddie could make things sound so good and logical when they really didn't make much sense at all if you thought about them. She looked up. "Where you been keeping the extra money, Eddie? There's no more in the egg jar than what I put there."

"Don't keep all your egg money in one jar, I say. I've got it in a safe place. Don't worry."

"Do you have enough for the trip now?"

"Almost," Eddie smiled. "Just sign this. We'll sell the rest of the animals tomorrow, and I think we'll have enough to leave the day after." His fingers gripped her shoulder tightly, digging into the soft flesh. He was getting impatient. She dipped the pen into the ink.

CHAPTER EIGHTEEN

Snake Patrol

Wednesday, April 20, 1921, Rockytop—*The cold, cruel winds of March have turned into warm gentle breezes in April. Too warm, the farmers say. We had a little rain the first of the month, but nothing since. Halpern Creek is up a little but not the raging torrent it was last spring. The farmers are getting worried there won't be enough irrigation water to last through the summer. The snowpack in the La Platas is down from last year. Where I used to live, if we had problems with precipitation, it was too much, not too little. I find myself worrying about the weather almost as much as the farmers do.*

I've also noticed that weather affects the mood of the classroom. Right before a storm, the children are much quieter than usual. During a storm, they're difficult to control—partly because storms are so rare they just have to go to the windows and watch. On nice spring days like we've been having, they're lazy. All they want to do is read or go outside and practice softball.

I had hoped Michael and Solly's cooperation at the fire would translate to cooperation on the softball field, but that hasn't happened. For a few days they were nicer to each other, but then Michael's resentment of Solly's pitching resurfaced and they are back to their old animosity. Even Angus is getting disgusted with them.

I had an interesting conversation with Richard the other day. He says that, after the fire, Sol decided to join the rest of the men in the night patrols. I hadn't realized it until Richard told me, but the Stonacres were about the last to know about the fire. Ethyl, who is a light sleeper, heard the bell ringing and woke Silas. They saw the flames and rushed over to the Stonacres'. They had to wake them up and help get the kids out of the house. If the fire hadn't been seen as soon as it was, they would have stayed asleep until the house caught on fire, and by then it might have been too late to get all the children out. I hope Sol is coming to realize the value of having neighbors who pay attention and are willing to help.

I asked Richard if Sol knew about Edmund, since that's the reason the patrols started. He said he didn't think so, that he just mentioned watching for fires and predators going after the livestock. I said not to tell him. I'm not sure Sol would protect me from Edmund anyway. I feel he doesn't like me, and he might take Edmund's side.

The Stonacre and Fredrickson children arrived at school in a state of excitement. "We saw two snakes on the road, just the other side of the bridge," Gunny reported. "Long ones."

"Rattlers?" Angus asked, looking up in alarm.

"Nah," Solly said, "just bull snakes. They was sunning themselves to warm up. Early for snakes to be out, Pa says, but we saw one on our place yesterday, too."

"I guess the warm weather has the snakes fooled, too," Robert said. "I wished I'd seen them. I would have caught them and brought them to school. They could be our mascots and help catch mice."

"On, no you wouldn't," Minta said. "No snakes allowed in school!"

"You afraid of snakes?" Michael asked, looking up in interest.

"No, I'm not," Minta said firmly. "But we have enough distractions around here without having to look where we put our feet all the time. Besides, Blackie does a fine job with the mice. She doesn't need any help from reptiles."

She finally got them settled down and working on their lessons—or as much as they worked on nice spring days, anyway. It was with relief that she sent them out to recess. She opened the windows to air out the classroom and bring in the fresh breezes. As she did so, she heard loud, argumentative voices from the playing field out back.

She walked out to the practice field in time to hear Angus say, "Will you two just shut up? Who cares who catches the ball as long as someone does. That's the point, isn't it? To catch the ball and get an out against the other team."

"Yeah, but I yelled 'it's mine,' and Solly jumped right in front of me and caught it," Michael said. "He thinks he has to do everything."

"I do not. The ball was going right over my head, so I just jumped up and caught it. I didn't hear you say it was yours."

"Yeah, I'll bet. Just stick to your pitching. You can almost do that."

"Michael," Minta said, "that will do. If you kids can't practice softball without arguing, I have some work you can do inside. Maybe we should cut recess short today."

"So you're going to punish everyone because Michael's acting like a weasel?" Gertie asked.

"Shut up, Gertie!" Michael yelled.

"That's Strike One, Michael," Minta said. "You know I don't like anyone to tell anyone else to shut up."

"Well, what about Angus? He's been telling us to shut up all day. Just because he's the coach, he can do it, but not me? You always take Angus and Solly's side."

"I'm not taking anyone's side. Angus and Solly aren't the ones arguing with me. You are. And I've had enough of it!"

"We were doing fine until you came out here and interfered. If you'd just . . ."

"Strike Two, Michael. I'd advise you to stop arguing, right now."

"Okay, everyone," Angus yelled. "Change up! Outfielders switch with the batters."

The children ran to their new positions. Minta turned and walked away. She smiled as she thought about Angus the peacemaker. Last year he'd been the troublemaker. She didn't see if Michael followed Angus's instructions, nor did she hear any more arguing. When she got inside, she wrote Michael's name on the board and added an X.

She tried to keep the students working diligently the rest of the day. She moved from student to student and didn't give anyone a chance to daydream or visit with a neighbor. The last class of the day was history for the older students and spelling and penmanship for the younger ones. She got the older ones started on their reading assignment in the history books and went to help the younger ones form their letters correctly.

As she was guiding Dale's hand across the page, she heard a commotion behind her and turned in time to see Michael launching a spitwad at the back of Solly's head.

"Michael!" she said. "Apologize to Solly, right now."

"What?! You didn't see what he did to me!"

"What have I told you? It's usually the second one who gets caught. If you don't want to get in trouble, you have to not retaliate when someone else starts something."

"So you're not going to do anything about him?" Michael asked.

"I can only handle what I can see. And I saw *you*. I guess that's Strike Two." She went to write an X on the board when she and Michael realized at the same time that is was really Strike Three. "I guess I mean Strike Three," she said, circling his name. "See me after school."

Shocked by the implications of a Third Strike, he didn't argue. And she only had the rest of the school day to decide what to do about him. She didn't send him to the chair in the cloakroom because, unlike the younger students, he would enjoy being out of the classroom.

After she dismissed the students for the day, Angus walked by Michael's desk. "We'll wait for you up by the first turn in the road." Minta knew that was so they could all return home at the same time. If the rest of them got there before Michael, it would be obvious to his parents that he'd been kept after school. If they were *all* a little late, their parents would just think she'd forgotten to dismiss them on time or that they'd been playing around on the way home. She was sure Angus would also be reminding the younger ones not to tattle.

She sat at her desk and looked at Michael sitting in his. She still hadn't decided for sure what to do, although she knew what Fred would expect her to do. Finally, the silence got to Michael and he said, "You're not going to whip me."

She had to fight not to smile. It was the same thing Angus had said last year. It hadn't worked for him, either. She made her decision.

"Whenever you're ready," she said, "go get me the ferule from the cupboard."

A chilly breeze came in the windows, and she went to close them. Then she sat back down at her desk and picked up her red pencil and a pile of papers to grade. She began grading the penmanship papers, although she knew she'd have to go over them all again. She wasn't really concentrating.

It was so quiet she could hear her own breathing, and Michael's. She cringed when the sound of Blackie wanting in at the window screeched into the silence. The cat knew when school was out and often came back to enjoy some quiet time with her. She got up to let Blackie in. As she passed Michael's desk, he was sitting, intently studying his fingernails. Well, she could wait as long as he could. Longer, really. Sooner or later Fred would come to see what was going on. Fred was the deal breaker here, and Michael knew it, just as Angus had last year. The price of refusing to cooperate with her was to face Fred.

As if reading her thoughts, Michael sighed, got up, and went to the cupboard.

The next day at morning recess the younger boys were teasing Michael and trying to get him to tell what had happened after school. Finally Solly said, "Will you blockheads leave off? If you want to know so bad, *you* get three strikes." That silenced them for a while, at least. Minta looked out the back door to see that they all seemed to have settled into practice.

She was just thinking it was time to ring the bell to call them in when she heard shouts and screams. She looked out to see a knot of kids clustered around Solly and Michael in a corner of the schoolyard. Because of the other children, she couldn't see what they were doing, but it looked for all the world like a fight. She had known it would come to this, sooner or later. She ran outside.

"Stay back, Miss Mayfield," Angus said. "It's dangerous. Don't get too close."

"Solly, Michael—come here!" She ordered.

"We can't, Teacher," Solly answered. "We got this snake here."

Finally the other students parted for her, and she saw Michael with a long stick poking at a rattlesnake that was coiled in the corner of the fence.

"All of you get back into the school," she ordered. As the kids started to move back, she turned and saw Angus's pale face. He was holding a shaking and sobbing Mary. Minta remembered it was a rattlesnake right near the school that had caused their father's death. "Angus, I need you to get Mary inside. And Clara, you help get all the others in. Angus and Clara are in charge until I come in. Now go!" She ordered the children.

She turned back to Solly and Michael. They still had the snake cornered. "Why aren't you letting it crawl away?" she asked.

"Do you really want us to do that?" Michael asked. "Then you'll always wonder where it is—like what you said about having to watch where we put our feet all the time."

"Yeah," Solly said. "We have to kill it. You got a gun?"

"No, I don't," Minta said. Last year she had vowed to get a gun in case Edmund came back. She'd even gone shopping for one in Liberty. But, once she was holding it in her hands, she knew she'd never be able to use it on another human being. Even Edmund.

"I seen my Pa kill a rattler with a shovel once," Solly said. "You got a shovel?"

"There's one in the woodshed," she said.

"Well, go get it," Michael and Solly said together. She didn't even mind taking orders from them.

She brought the shovel back and handed it to Solly. "Now what?"

"Okay, here's what we'll do," he said. "Michael, you keep it distracted with that stick, and I'll get it with the shovel."

"I don't know if I can allow you to do that," Minta said. "It sounds dangerous."

"The stick's longer than the snake," Michael said. "Even if it strikes toward me, I won't get bit as long as I stay a stick-length away. And its attention will be on me. Solly can get it from behind."

She watched as the boys put their plan into action. It did strike at Michael who jumped back, and as soon as it was stretched out full-length, Solly brought the shovel blade down and cut it cleanly in two. Just to make sure, he severed it a couple more times. Minta closed her eyes at the gore, then forced them open again. It wouldn't do to show weakness at this point.

"Thank you," she said. "You boys did a good job. I'm proud of both of you. Now go bury it somewhere. I don't want Blackie dragging pieces of it in like she does mice and birds."

Solly started to gather up the still-writhing pieces with the shovel.

"Wait," Michael said, taking out his pocketknife. "We have to cut off the rattles." He bent down to the tail section and cut them off. "Look, three segments, just a three-year-old," he said, holding up the rattles. Then he looked at Solly and held out his hand. "Here," he said, "it's your kill, your rattles."

"Thanks," Solly said, pocketing the prize.

"Wash your hands when you come in," Minta said, leaving them to their task.

When they returned to the classroom, she let them show the rattles and tell the other students how they had disposed of the rattlesnake. Then she had them explain how to tell a snake's age by the number of rattles. "Every time the snake sheds its skin," Michael explained, "a new set of rattles grows. The more rattles, the older the snake."

And she made a new rule. The new rule was that Michael and Solly got to get out for recess a few minutes early every day to check the playground and practice field for snakes. Only when they said it was okay to go out could the rest of the children leave the schoolroom. Their new job title became Snake Patrol.

CHAPTER NINETEEN

Visitors in Liberty

Liberty Colorado, April 1920

Mr. and Mrs. Edward Smith strolled the streets of Liberty. They'd
arrived the day before and spent the night in the only hotel. The lady
at the desk, Mrs. Whiteside, had been most helpful. She was more than
willing to answer any question at great length. And she seemed to know
everything about everyone in town.

Sari looked up at Eddie as they walked along. She knew they were
going to talk to a man about property. Mrs. Whiteside helpfully
pointed out just where the surveyor's office was and said he'd know if
there was any of the type of property they were looking for available.
Eddie had warned Sari to let him do all the talking. If anyone asked
her questions, she was just to give short answers or none at all if she
wasn't sure what it was safe to say.

They had on new clothes they'd bought in Kansas City—the nicest
clothes she'd ever owned. Maybe it wouldn't be so bad being Mrs.
Eddie Smith. The hotel room was clean and comfortable, and having
someone else prepare all their meals was a luxury she never thought
she'd have.

They stopped outside the door of the surveyor's office and Eddie
gripped her arm. "Remember what I told you!" he whispered. She nodded. They went inside to the tinkling of a bell over the door. A man

came out of a back room and asked if he could help them. She felt Eddie stiffen and heard the sharp intake of his breath. He covered his discomfort with a fit of coughing, his hand to his mouth.

"Are you all right?" the man asked. "Could I get you some water?"

"No, thank you," Eddie said. "Please excuse me. My lungs aren't as young as they used to be." Sari didn't know why Eddie was always wanting to act like an old man. She'd heard Mrs. Whiteside telling someone that her new guests were an older couple in their fifties. Why, Sari wasn't much over forty, and she didn't think Eddie was even that old. But Eddie had laughed and said, "Wonderful! Perfect!" when she told him what Mrs. Whiteside said.

"I'm Matthew Post." The man extended his hand to Eddie. "How may I help you?"

Eddie shook his hand. "Edward Smith. And my wife, Sarah. The kind lady at the hotel said you might be able to point us in the direction of available farm ground. I see you have a lot of maps. Maybe you could show us where to look."

"Well, all the land that was free for proving-up has been taken. But there's some parcels for sale. People tend to find out that free land isn't all that free once they get settled in and the real work begins. You looking for dryland or irrigated?"

"I'd consider either," Eddie said. "I haven't really decided."

"If you're a gambler, go with the dryland. It's a lot cheaper but a lot riskier. In a bad year, like this one, you might not get enough rain to bring your crops in." He walked over to a map hanging on the wall. "There are quite a few places for sale over on what we call the Dryside—other side of the Liberty River—too high to irrigate and very few wells worth the name. There's some fellers trying to raise pinto beans and grass hay over there, but like I said, it's risky."

Eddie had wandered over to the wall and was looking at some photographs. "Are you interested in schools, Mr. Post? I see you have several pictures of school buildings."

"Yes. Besides being a surveyor, I'm the Superintendent of Schools."

"This is an interesting setting," Eddie said, pointing at one of the pictures. "What's this school called?"

"That's Rockytop. It *is* an interesting place. I know I shouldn't have favorites among all the schools, but I'd have to admit Rockytop's my favorite. Of course, it doesn't look quite like that any more." Mr. Post walked over to the wall and pointed. "The teacherage—this building here—burned down last year, and the school itself was damaged. It's now been repaired and a bedroom added on for the teacher."

"Is that right?" Eddie said. "How convenient! For her, I mean. I'm assuming it's a woman. They usually are, aren't they?"

"Mostly. We do have a man at Halpern. But Rockytop's teacher is a lovely young woman. I'm not sure how 'convenient' she's finding the added-on room, however. I know it's not as nice for her as when she had her own cabin." He looked at his watch. "Didn't you say you were interested in land?"

"Yes. Is there any out toward this Rockytop place? From this picture here, it looks like an area I might be interested in."

Mr. Post pulled out another map and spread it on a table. "This was the last land opened up for homesteading," he said. "A lot of the original owners gave up after a few hard years. Several families are still holding on. None of the places right around Rockytop are for sale. There are two places downstream—that's the Halpern Creek there— between Rockytop and Halpern. That's irrigated land, but I wouldn't count on getting water every year. The places upstream have first rights, so you'd only get what's left over, if anything."

"I might want to look at those places," Eddie said. "Could you show me the best way to get there?"

"What about your wife? She hasn't said anything." Mr. Post turned to Sari. "Do you think you'd like living way out in the middle of nowhere? It's a pretty hard life. The road isn't fit to use except in dry weather, and neighbors are few and far between."

Sari looked up from where she'd been studying her shoes wondering just what Eddie was after. "Oh!" she said. "Well, I . . ."

"She'll be fine wherever we go. Won't you dear?" Eddie's eyes bored into her.

"Oh, yes, fine. Wherever we go."

The surveyor man frowned. "I don't mean to be insulting, but I have to warn you. If you're looking for an out of the way place to set up a still, I'd advise you to go elsewhere. Our sheriff, Mo Upton, does-n't look the other way like a lot of them do. He'll find it, destroy it, and run you in."

Eddie tried to look indignant. "Of course not! I'm interested in farm ground and that's all!"

"Well, if that's the case then, there's two ways to get out toward Rockytop. There's this back trail," Mr. Post traced it with his fingers, "but you can't take a vehicle there. Or the main road through Halpern. Turn up Halpern Creek right by the church and go to Tin Can Corner. You'll recognize it because there's a post with cans nailed to it for the Rockytop mail. That's as far as an automobile can go. So you'll have to park and walk from there or take a horse or wagon. The first place is one mile past the corner on the left. The other one's a half mile further on up stream on the right. You can borrow this map as long as you bring it back." He penciled in Xs on the map where the two properties were.

Outside the shop, Eddie tucked the map under his arm, laughed, and bent down and kissed Sari full on the lips.

"Eddie! Sorry, I mean Edward. What are you doing? It's broad day-light."

"He didn't recognize me. Not even a glimmer. It's going to work this time. I know it."

"You know that man?"

"I met him last year. I was a little startled when I realized who he was, but he didn't have any idea who I was. And he thought I wanted to set up a still and make hootch. That's rich! Let them think that! I'm sure my plan will work now."

"You was here last year? When?"

"Right before I . . . came to your place. Enough questions. We've got work to do."

A young man said, "Excuse me," and walked past them. Eddie grabbed her arm and jerked her close to him. "Quick! That man that just passed! Watch where he goes and what he does and tell me everything." Eddie turned his back to the man and positioned Sari facing down the street where he'd gone.

"He's going into a store," Sari said.

"What store? What's the name of it?"

"There's a sign, but you know I cain't read it. Look fur yourself."

"What's in the window? What kind of store does it look like?"

"There's a display of fancy hats in one window. The other has sewing notions, looks like."

"Okay. Wait and tell me when he comes out and where he goes next. I wouldn't think a man would spend too much time in a store with ladies' hats and sewing notions. He must have to pick up something for his wife."

"How do you know he's got a wife?" Sari asked. "You know him, too?"

"I sure never expected to find them here," Eddie said under his breath. "I guess it makes sense, though. They'd all stick together. That complicates things, but it might turn out for the best."

"What . . ." Sari started to ask, but Eddie shushed her.

They waited a long time, but the man never came out. Finally Eddie got impatient, and people were starting to look at them as though wondering why they were just standing on the street corner. "We're going into that store," Eddie said. "You might have to do some talking. We'll pretend we want to buy you a hat. Just follow my lead."

They walked down the street and across to the store. Inside, the man was waiting on a customer. "Ah," Eddie said. "It's *his* store—or he works here." They looked at bolts of material until the customer left. As the man approached them, Eddie turned sideways and put his hand partly over his face as if scratching his chin.

"Good day. May I help you?" the man asked.

"Yes, we're looking for a summer hat for my wife," Eddie said.

"You came to the right place. My wife makes the best hats in town." He led them to a corner of the shop set up with a work area for hat-making. Completed hats were displayed on a freestanding coat rack. "She's upstairs taking care of the baby right now, but if you need to consult with her, I'll go get her."

Sari heard the sudden intake of breath and felt Eddie grip her arm when the man said "the baby," but he recovered enough to say, "No. That won't be necessary. Just try a few of these on, dear."

Sari tried on hats while Eddie found something wrong with each one: wrong color, too many feathers, not enough feathers, too heavy for summer, and so forth. She wondered what he was up to.

"I know these aren't the most up-to-date," the man said, "but most of the women here prefer these older styles. It seems it takes the West a few years to catch up with the rest of the country in fashion. Are you sure you don't want me to go get my wife? She could make one to your order with the color and type of feathers you want."

"Maybe some other time," Eddie said. "Come along, dear. We'll be late to our appointment."

"What app . . ." Sari started to say. A sharp poke in her side silenced her.

Outside Eddie could hardly contain his glee. "He didn't recognize me either! And his wife has a baby! How interesting. We need to find out more about that."

"Eddie, you are a piece of work. What do we care about some hat lady's baby?"

"You might come to care very much, Sarah, dear. I know how you're hankering to have another baby. You may be closer than you think."

"You know I'm not in the family way, Eddie. I'm afraid I'm getting too old. Maybe we should just forget about having a baby."

"There's more than one way to get a baby. We may be here a little longer than I thought. Now, we need to go talk to that helpful Mrs. Whiteside again."

CHAPTER TWENTY

Be Careful What You Wish For

༺≫≪༻

Sunday, May 8, 1921, Liberty—*The school year is fast coming to a close. I'll have to quit spending so much time in Liberty if I'm to get everything done I need to do before I close the book on another year. I love spending time with Lulabelle and little Frankie. He's getting so cute now that he spends more time awake and can smile and laugh and sit up. His hair is still thick and black, but I think Lulabelle almost doesn't notice it any more. His eyes are still blue.*

I'm going to attend church with the Posts this morning, have lunch with Frank and Lulabelle, then head back to Rockytop. I'll be glad to get back to the peace and quiet there. Oh, I hear Miriam in the kitchen. I'd better go help with breakfast.

"How was church?" Lulabelle asked as Minta helped her set the table for lunch.

"Oh, fine, but I'd rather hear Reverend MacIntosch's sermons in Halpern. I do wish you'd come to church with us, Lulabelle."

"Oh, we go sometimes. Usually the weekends when you're not here. But when you *are* here, I like to spend more time with you and fix lunch for us."

"Lulabelle Elizabeth! Don't you dare use me as an excuse for not going to church!"

"Oh, I didn't mean it that way. You know I've never been as keen on going every week as you. It just seems there's always so much else that needs to be done."

"The day of rest . . ." Minta started to say.

Lulabelle laughed. "Look outside, Minta. Who do you see resting?"

"That's why I'm always so glad to get home to Rockytop. Liberty is just too busy. There's always noise and commotion and . . ."

"And excitement." Lulabelle finished for her.

"I'm not sure I'd call what goes on here exciting."

"Well, it's not exciting enough for me," Lulabelle declared. "In fact, I wish . . ."

"Be careful what you . . ." Minta started to warn.

"Don't tell me to be careful what I wish for! I'll wish for whatever I want. In fact, I wish . . . I wish that something *wickedly* exciting would happen. So there!"

Minta shook her head and sighed. Sometimes dealing with Lulabelle was like dealing with one of her students. "Let's change the subject. What have you been working on downstairs?"

"Oh, I have a custom order for a hat. This woman, Mrs. Smith, has been coming in every day for fittings. She always wants something changed. I don't think I'm ever going to get it done to suit her. And all she does is ask me questions. How old is my baby? When was he born exactly? What does he look like? I get tired talking to her."

"Maybe she likes to visit. She sounds like a lonely widow."

"No, she's got a husband. I've never seen him, but Frank did the first day they came into the store. Frank didn't like them but encouraged her to order a hat from me anyway. He thinks I need to make and sell hats for my own good, or something."

"Well, the doctor did say that it would be good therapy for you."

"Sure, back when I was still recovering. But I'm fine now, in case you haven't noticed."

"You are a lot better since you moved here. Of course, I didn't see you before . . ."

"I suppose it could also be because we need the money. Frank doesn't talk much about finances, but I know he worries about everything. If I can help out by selling the hats, I will. And I'll charge that Smith woman a pretty penny for hers."

Minta returned to Rockytop with renewed vigor to make the last weeks of school productive. The last day of instruction would be Thursday, May 27th, with the all-school picnic and softball tournament the next day at Halpern.

She was pleased with the new cooperation between Michael and Solly, and not just on the softball field. Funny that a snake could bring them together in a way she couldn't. She complimented them every chance she got on how well they worked together and let them work on their lessons together, too. Michael was turning into a good tutor for Solly without Solly realizing he was being tutored like he did when she tried to have Clara work with him.

Minta was afraid Angus was now feeling like the odd man out and approached him one day to ask him. "No," he said, "school's almost over. I'm going to graduate—I hope. I won't be back next year, and they will. It's better they get along with each other. And I still have Michael at home. Spending all my time with him at school would be too much. You know how he is."

Minta laughed. "I sure do. What are you going to do after you graduate? Which, by the way, I'm sure you will. You've made real progress with your lessons this year."

"I don't know. I don't want to go to high school. I think I'll go to Durango and see if I can get a job somewhere. Mother doesn't want me to go into the Liberty Mine, but I'd like to have some money to give to her and Mary to make life a little easier for them. Uncle Fred's been good to us, but sometimes we feel like we're taking charity from him. Do you really think I can pass the exams? I'm worried about the English part, especially."

"Yes, Angus, I *know* you can do it. We'll work some more these last two weeks on writing essays and on other things you feel a little unsure about. In fact, I have some sample questions I got from a teacher in Liberty last year for you to practice on."

"Like what?"

"They're in my desk inside, but I remember one from the history section that asks you to name the principle campaigns and military leaders of the Civil War. I'll bet you can do that."

"Yeah, I like history. Now. What else is on there?" Angus asked.

"One of the essay questions says to write two hundred words on the evil effects of alcoholic beverages."

"Only two hundred? I'd just have to remember the opening of one of Uncle Fred's lectures."

Minta laughed.

"Miss Mayfield?" Angus looked down at the floor.

"Yes, Angus, what is it?"

"I just want to thank you for coming here and being my teacher. If you hadn't, I don't think I'd be graduating at all. I probably would have dropped out by now."

"What a nice thing to say, Angus. But it's I who need to thank you—all of my students. You taught me how to be a teacher."

"I thought that's what your teacher school did."

"They taught us a lot of things, like how to do lesson plans and how to write properly on the blackboard. But teaching is something you can only learn by doing."

Minta was still smiling a half hour after Angus left. She remembered something one of her Normal School instructors had said about the rewards of teaching. They were few and far between, but each successful student, each word of praise received from a student or parent, each smile from a student who usually frowned made you forget all the bad days and made teaching worthwhile.

The next day the Stonacre children were late. Again. All their varied excuses for being late had become a class joke.

"To what major catastrophe do we owe your tardiness?" Minta asked with a twinkle in her eye as they filed into their seats. "Pigs get out? Cows refusing to give milk? Chickens all aflutter?"

There were more than a few giggles. The children loved it when she teased. But still, they knew promptness was one of the values she tried to teach them.

"Sorry, ma'am," Solly said. "We got held up by Uncle Ed and Aunt Sarah. Oh, I don't mean like they held us up with a gun or nothing. But they stopped us on the road and wanted to talk."

"Who are Uncle Ed and Aunt Sarah?" Minta asked.

"They've been camping out at our place a few days, up on the high pasture. They like to look out over the whole valley. They're looking to buy land hereabouts. He's even got one of those spyglass things that makes far away stuff look close up. He let me look through it, and I could even see the patched place on the school roof and the rope on the bell."

"Are they relatives on your father's side or mother's?" Minta asked.

"I don't know. They just told us to call them Aunt and Uncle."

"Well, you can't allow them to make you late for school. If they want to talk to you, they can do it when you're home."

"Yes'm. We tried to tell them that," Clara said.

Everett laughed. "But Uncle Ed said we shouldn't listen to any dumb teacher." The rest of the class laughed.

"But we said you wasn't dumb," Eleanor quickly added. "Then he asked us a lot of questions about you and how school was going and what we did every day."

"Weren't dumb," Minta corrected. "All right. They wasted your time on the way to school and they've wasted enough of our time here. I don't want to hear any more about them. Let's get busy."

After school Minta walked over to visit Claudia. Whenever she got to missing Frankie, she went over to spend some time with Meg. She was finding she had a real love of babies. Meg was less than two months older than Frankie, but she seemed so much bigger and more developed.

"I love seeing what Meg does," Minta told Claudia, "so I can be ready for Frankie's next accomplishments."

"Well, I love you coming to play with Meg, so I can get something else done. Do you mind if I punch down my bread dough and make it into rolls while we talk?"

"Do whatever you need to do. Of course, if we talk long enough I might still be here when the fresh rolls come out of the oven." Minta bounced Meg on her knee.

"I expect you to stay for supper, Minta."

"Oh, I didn't mean to invite myself for dinner. I'm sorry. How rude of me!"

"You could never be rude, Minta. Even if you tried—it just wouldn't work. Not like those people staying over at Ruby's."

"The kids were talking about them—they called them Uncle Ed and Aunt Sarah. Are they rude? Have you met them?"

"No, but Ruby's not real happy about them staying at their place. They're camping out in a tent, so mostly just use their well and outhouse, but they're always bothering the kids when they should be doing chores." Claudia floured the table and dumped the bread dough onto it.

"I know. They made the kids late for school today. Wonder what they're doing here? Most people who want to camp go up in the La Platas."

"Ruby says they're thinking of buying land around here and want to stay here a while to get to know the area and see if they like it."

Minta was fascinated at how fast Claudia could pinch off a piece of dough and form it into a perfect roll. "Why doesn't she like them?" Minta asked. "It looks like she'd enjoy having another woman to talk to."

"She says the woman doesn't talk much, just the man. And she doesn't like him. She didn't really say why. Said they were paying Sol to camp there, which is why Sol let them stay."

"Oh? I thought they were relatives. The kids call them aunt and uncle."

"I don't know. Sol's the type that would even charge relatives to stay."

"Tight with the money, is he?" Minta asked. "Like Edmund."

"He may be tight, but I don't think he's as much like Edmund as you think he is, Minta. At least he has a respect for the law and wants to do right by his family, even if he goes about it the wrong way sometimes. But let's not argue about Sol. What were we talking about? Oh, those people camping. I don't think they have any kids, so even if they do buy land, you won't have an increase in enrollment."

"Well, they didn't pick a very good year to look at land here," Minta said. "Everything's so dry and withered that I wouldn't think anyone would seriously consider buying a place."

"Probably think they can get something real cheap. That's what happens in bad years."

"Well, that's their problem. I don't want to talk about them, either. Tell me about Meg's latest accomplishments—any new teeth?" Minta stuck her finger in Meg's mouth to look.

"Careful, you'll get bit," Claudia said just as Minta cried, "Ouch! You wait, little girl. Some day I'll be your teacher and I'll get even with you."

"Oh, I hope you will be, Minta. Do you really think you'll stay here that long? Even with it so dried up and withered?"

"I love it here, Claudia. I'll stay as long as you'll have me, until *I'm* all dried up and withered."

Chapter Twenty-One

Trusting Eddie

❦

Liberty Colorado, May 1921

Eddie had been on edge all day. Sari wasn't sure whether talking to him would make him better or worse. One or the other, though. She was glad they weren't staying in that hot tent anymore. There was nothing to do there except watch Eddie look through the spyglass. Mostly he looked at the school and the teacher. Sometimes he turned in the opposite direction and watched the man who had the ranch next to the Stonacres'. He didn't seem to like that man for some reason. They hadn't even met him. Eddie went out of his way to avoid him if they saw him coming down the road.

Sari hoped their stay in Colorado was almost over. Eddie got more excited and hard to get along with each day. He was building up to something; she just didn't know what. Once they were married and settled down somewheres like he promised, he'd be a lot better, she hoped. He just needed a good, steady woman like her to get him back on track, not like that woman he was trying to get free of. He was a hard worker; she would say that for him. And he knew how to get things done.

Now they were back in town. Eddie had promised to tell her everything tonight. Tomorrow was the big day, he said. Whatever that meant. Right now she was supposed to be going to the hat lady's place to tell her that she'd be in tomorrow to pick up the hat and pay for it. She was supposed to find out when the lady would be there and where she'd be the rest of the day. Eddie didn't tell her how to find that out, but she knew she had to do it.

It turned out to be easier than she thought. She just asked and was told. It was like the lady was telling her whatever she wanted to know just to get rid of her. But Sari wasn't going to tell Eddie everything *he* wanted to know until he answered some questions for her.

They met back in their room at the hotel.

"How did it go?" Eddie said. "What did you find out?"

"A lot," she said. "But first I want to know something. I want to know how you been paying for everything—this hotel, them clothes in Kansas City, all that camping stuff, the train, hiring a horse and buggy, the money you been giving that Sol. I know the egg money and what you sold wouldn't pay for all that."

Eddie turned his cold, hard eyes on her. He waited a long time before answering. Finally he said, "You're right, Sarah. I needed more money than we were ever going to be able to scrape up at your place. That's why I sold it."

"You . . . *what*?" She'd been expecting him to say anything but that. Maybe that he'd had some savings he hadn't told her about or even that he'd robbed a bank. How could he have sold her place?

"You heard me. I sold it. You know those papers I had you sign? That was the bill of sale. I left one copy on the table for the new owners and told them they could move in the next day."

"But what about Orville?" Sari wailed. "That place was for Orville!"

"Who cares? Maybe the new owners will adopt him. Not if they've got half a brain, though."

"But . . . but if you sold the place, where will we go?"

"Sarah, Sari . . . listen to me. I know it's scary to think about going someplace new, but that's what we have to do. We're going to start a new life—just you and me and our baby."

"What baby? I'm not . . ."

"It's time you know what's going on," Eddie said. "Here. Sit down." He held one of her hands in his, gently, not bone-crushing like he usually did. "I promised to marry you, and I will, so that you can take care of my . . . our baby. Everything is going to work out fine, if you'll just help me through this last part. It's for *our* future."

Sari was too stunned to speak. He continued, "The lady who makes hats is the mother of my baby. She's trying to keep him from me, but I'm going to get him back, and you and I will raise him up as our own. I need sons to help me with farming. Maybe we'll have a few more together." He slid his hand across her stomach and up to her breasts like he did when he wanted to lie with her. She wasn't in the mood.

"*She's* your wife?" Sari was confused. "Then why does she think she's married to the dry goods man?"

"No, no! She's not my wife, just the mother of my baby."

So Eddie had been with more women than her. She guessed she shouldn't be surprised. "Is that why you always make me go talk to her alone?" she asked.

"Yes, there are only two people here who might recognize me, even as changed as I am, and she's one of them."

"Who's the other one?"

"The teacher at that school across the valley from where we were camping. That lying, stealing bitch . . . *she's* my wife."

"Then why didn't you go talk to her about getting a divorce while we was out there? I thought that's what we come for."

"I never said anything about a divorce. I said I was going to fix it so I was free to marry you, and I am. I needed to see if she was still here, where she was living, and make my plans. I've done that now. It took longer than I thought once I found out Lulabelle was here and had a baby. But now . . ."

"Lulabelle?"

"The hat lady. Stupid name, isn't it? It fits her." Eddie stood up and paced across the room.

"Eddie, you're scaring me," Sari said. "What are you going to do? How are you going to get the baby? Does that Lulabelle want to give him to you?"

He turned suddenly and walked back to her, towering over her, his hands on his hips. "What did you find out from her today?" he asked. She could tell it was time to stop stalling and tell him. When he got that look in his eye, it wasn't a good idea to cross him.

"She'll be working on hats in the morning. She said I can go in, pick up the hat, and pay her there. Then after lunch she's going to take the baby walking in his stroller to put him to sleep for his nap. Then . . ."

"Stop. That's enough. That will do fine."

"Eddie, I'm not sure I want to do whatever it is you're planning."

"You have no choice now, Sari. You have no home to go back to— no home but with me. Stick with me and I'll take care of you for the rest of your life. You'll have a beautiful baby boy right away and more to follow if we're lucky. We'll move on to California. I've got enough left from the sale of the place to get us started somewhere. I'm a good farmer, a hard worker; we'll do all right. Much better than you were doing in Missouri."

"But what about your wife? How are you goin' to get shut of her?"

Eddie's eyes got even blacker. They looked like pools of oil. His mouth twitched as if the words were trying to get out. Finally he said, "She ruined my life. Because of her I lost my wealth, my farm, my family, my youth. Because of her I look like an old man and have injuries that will pain me the rest of my days. She doesn't deserve to live on this Earth any more. Her or that cowboy boyfriend of hers." He slapped his hand down on the dresser, making the wash basin jump, and Sari, too. He looked back at her and his eyes had lightened up a little. The corners of his mouth turned up. "It's nice the little pretend teacher and her cowboy puppy dog see so little of each other these days. It won't be hard to get to them separately. This time."

"Oh, Eddie . . ." Could he see the terror in her eyes? What was he going to do?

"Shhh, Sari. Don't say anything. Just leave everything to me. If you don't know what all I'm planning, you won't have to worry about it. Just think about how you're going to love that little baby. Now, I want you to go buy what you need to take care of him for several days until we get away from here. Be sure and tell the store people you're buying baby gifts for a relative." He took her shoulders in his hands, pulled her to him, and kissed her roughly. She thought he'd want more as he usually did, but he didn't. He just released her and gave her money to go buy the baby things.

When Sari got back, Eddie told her what the plans were for the next day and what her part was to be. He made it very clear she didn't have a choice. Well, she did, he implied. The other choice would be to join his soon to be ex-wife in her fate. Even when Eddie was at his maddest, Sari had never seen him as mad as he'd been when talking about his wife. She hoped she would never make him that mad, so mad that he could barely talk. He was a volcano, and tomorrow would be the eruption.

While shopping for the baby things, Sari had briefly considered running away from Eddie. But where would she go? How would she get more money? She had no place to go back to, no way to earn money. She couldn't even read and write. Eddie was right. Her best chance was to stick with him. And, after she helped him tomorrow, he'd be indebted to her. She'd just have to trust him. Now that was a scary thought—trust Eddie.

CHAPTER TWENTY-TWO

Playing With Fire

꙳

Friday, May 13, 1921, Rockytop—*Friday the 13th! The students were talking today about all the bad things that might happen. They didn't even want Blackie to come in. Good thing I'm not superstitious. I'm going to stay here this weekend to get all the end-of-school tests ready and to work on my record books for the school board. I guess I'll try to find a job in Liberty for the summer. I would love to spend a summer at Rockytop but, without my monthly teacher's pay, I'd be dependent on the charity of the residents. I couldn't put them out like that. Maybe one of these years I'll have enough saved up that I can stay on my own for the summer. At least now I can save and control my own money, something Edmund would never let me do.*

I'm almost sure that Edmund is dead. He would have found his way back here by now if he weren't. I know he wouldn't have forgotten about me, even knowing he's a wanted man here. Once he decides he has to have something, nothing will deter him. I'm even daring to hope that I'll eventually be able to have him legally declared dead, and then maybe Silas and I —well, if Silas still wants to by then. I haven't seen much of him lately. He hasn't been nearly as persistent in his pursuit of me as he was last year. "Out of sight, out of mind," Grandmother used to say. Lately, though, it's been hard to keep him out of my mind. I thought I had come to terms with the fact that I'd never be free to marry again. Why, now, am I questioning that and building up what may well be false hopes? That's another of Grandmother's favorites: "Hope springs eternal." I hope Silas really will wait for me as he said he would. I know he's busy on the ranch, and he has his mother for company so isn't

*as lonely as he used to be. Now, I'm the one who is lonely. How silly! How can I
be lonely with sixteen children—who will be here way too soon? I'd better get busy.*

Friday seemed to fly by. All sixteen students were present, a rarity.
Minta kept busy keeping them busy. She stayed inside during afternoon recess to grade papers. The happy sounds of children getting
along with each other came through in the open window, and she
hummed as she graded. It reminded her of last year. She hadn't realized
how consumed she'd been this year with discipline problems and the
need to get the Stonacre children caught up to grade level. She'd forgotten to take time just to enjoy the kids as they were. She decided to
give them, and herself, a few extra minutes of recess. Finally, she picked
up the hand bell and went to ring them in.

Silas was leaning on the fence watching softball practice. She stood
still and watched. Occasionally he would yell some advice or encour-
agement to one of the children. When Gina's turn at bat came up, he
vaulted the fence and went to show her how to hold the bat and how
to swing without toppling herself over as she usually did. Minta should
have asked Silas to come and help coach the team. It was obvious he
would enjoy it. Maybe next year.

No one had noticed her come out, so intent were they on their
game. She rang the bell to a chorus of groans and "not yets." Her
answer was to ring it again. They knew if she had to ring it a third time,
they would be in trouble. Reluctantly Mary, followed by the rest, began
the trek back to the school. Minta sent them inside to wash their hands
while she stayed to speak with Silas.

"I think you've got a good shot at beating Halpern this year," he
said. "Angus, Michael, and Solly are a real triple-threat, especially now
that they're playing together like a real team."

"Yes, I know. But winning isn't the most important thing."

"Are you trying to convince me or yourself? I know you'd love to
show up Ben Griffith."

"Is it that obvious? I know that's not a good motive, but that little man just rubs me the wrong way."

Silas laughed. "He's a pip-squeak all right, but a good man. To keep teaching that rough Halpern bunch for as long as he has . . ."

"I know," Minta said. "I guess I'm just jealous of anyone who might be a better teacher."

"No one could be a better teacher than you, Minta." He took her upper arms in his hands and looked into her face. They were almost exactly the same height. She loved his earnest blue-green eyes, so different from Edmund's, and the way he cocked his head a little when he smiled his lopsided smile, as if he were making up for the imbalance.

She blushed, afraid her admiration for him showed in her eyes. "Silas, please. The children will see." She tried to wriggle out of his grasp, but not very hard.

"What will they see? That I love you? I've never made a secret of that."

"I have to go in now, Silas. If I'm such a great teacher, I shouldn't be standing outside mooning over a cowboy while the children are doing who knows what inside."

Silas laughed. "I haven't heard any commotion inside. They're probably just trying to peek out the windows. But don't worry, we're too close to the building for them to see me kiss you." He pulled her quickly to him and kissed her full on the mouth.

When she finally broke away, breathless and hot, she turned to go inside. She didn't say anything. There was nothing to say and, besides, she didn't trust her voice.

"Meet me tonight, Minta," he said. "At dusk in that grove of cottonwoods you like down by the creek."

"I don't know . . ." She hesitated and turned back to face him.

"Please, Minta." He sounded like her students begging for extra time at recess. She was much better at turning *them* down.

"All right," she said, although she knew she shouldn't. No good could come of a married woman secretly meeting a single man at night in a secluded spot. Then why did the idea feel so good and warm inside her? "Little girls who play with fire are going to get burned," she could almost hear her grandmother say.

"See you tonight, Minta," Silas said softly as she turned away again.

When she reentered the classroom, students scurried to their chairs amid giggles and whispers. "Can't I even step outside the school for a minute without you misbehaving?" she said crossly. "Whose name is going on the board?"

The giggles and whispers stopped, and heads were bent over textbooks they were pretending to read. She could just imagine the inflated versions of Silas' visit their parents would be hearing tonight. Tonight—while she was in the cottonwood grove with . . .

She forced herself to think about the lessons she'd planned for the afternoon. "No one could be a better teacher than you," he'd said. She'd have to work hard the rest of today to prove it.

Chapter Twenty-three

Deception

✎

Liberty Colorado, May 13

Sari went over Eddie's instructions in her head. He said she had to get it all right the first time. She wouldn't get a second chance. And, if she failed, she'd have to face Eddie—a very mad Eddie.

She waited on the sidewalk until she saw the hat lady come out of the dry goods store pushing the baby in the carriage just like she'd said she would. Sari waited until they were almost to her and then waved her handkerchief and called out, "Oh, Mrs. Jackson. There you are. I'm sorry I didn't come this morning like I said I would."

The lady looked annoyed. She probably thought she wasn't ever going to get paid for that hat. Which she wasn't, in fact. She stopped pushing the carriage and turned to Sari.

"I have to get the money from my husband," Sari said. "He's just around back here in the alley with our horse and buggy. If you'd like to come with me, we can pay you and . . ."

"But I don't have the hat with me."

"That's okay. I'll come get it later. But I'd like to get you paid while my husband's available." She had memorized the words to say like Eddie taught her so she didn't sound like an "uneducated hillbilly" as Eddie put it.

"All right," Lulabelle said. She bent down and checked on the baby, adjusting his blanket. "It's too rough to push the buggy in the alley. I'll carry him," she said, picking up the baby. They stepped off the walk-way and walked toward the alley. No one else was around because it was still the lunch hour.

As soon as they turned the corner, they could see Eddie lying on the ground by the horse and buggy with his back to them, holding his leg and moaning. "Oh, dear!" Sari said. "He must have slipped with his cane and fallen again. Please, help me get him up."

"Shouldn't I go for the doctor?" Lulabelle started to turn back toward the street.

Sari grabbed her arm. "No! Don't do that. This happens all the time. We just need to stand him back up. He'll be all right. Lay the baby in the buggy for a minute so's you can help me."

The two women bent down on each side of the groaning man. He kept his face toward Sari as he sat up and put his arms around their shoulders. They helped him up to a standing position. He let go of Sari, who ran to the buggy as he'd told her to do, but kept his other arm tightly around Lulabelle's shoulder. Sari looked back and saw Lulabelle try to pull away, but he tightened his grip and turned to look at her. As soon as her eyes met his, she seemed to recognize him and opened her mouth to scream. He reached into his pocket and pulled out an ether-soaked rag with his free hand, placing it over her mouth and nose. He had visited the doctor last week, supposedly about his bum leg, but really to see where the ether was kept and to make sure no one else was working in the office. He returned later, when the doctor was out on a house call, and helped himself. He laughed about the trusting people out here in the West. Few doors were ever locked.

Sari had followed Eddie's detailed instructions and, as Lulabelle lost consciousness and slumped against him, Sari was already tying her ankles together with the rope that had been stashed in the buggy. Then she tied her hands behind her back, and Eddie lifted the now-uncon-scious woman into the buggy, laying her on the floor in front of the back seat. Before covering her with the blanket, he tied a gag around her mouth.

Sari picked up Frankie and his blanket and climbed into the front seat with Eddie who was grinning from ear to ear. "Clockwork, Sarah. That went like clockwork. Now, we've got to get to Rockytop on time. Hang on to that baby good. Here we go."

She gripped the baby tighter as the buggy jerked into motion. Her heart felt like horses were running across it and her hands were shaking. The baby started to squirm and fuss. She focused her attention on him. "It's okay, little Frankie," she cooed. "I guess I'm gonna be your mama now."

Eddie turned to her as he guided the horse onto the main road. "His name isn't Frankie. It's Edward. Edward Junior. Don't you forget it. And what do you mean, you *guess*? You damn well are his mama now. And I'm his father. Of course, I always have been."

"Yes, Eddie." Sari tried to placate him. His voice was rising in anger.

"And don't you be calling him Eddie. Or me, either. I'm Edward, too, now, or Ed. After today, Eddie no longer exists, just like Edmund."

"Who's Edmund?"

"Never you mind. Now, do you remember what you're supposed to do when we get out there?"

"I thought I was just sposed to stay with the buggy and take care of Frank . . . Eddie . . . Junior."

"That's right. You've got to keep him quiet, too. Use the ether rag, if you have to."

"Is that safe for a baby?"

"There won't be much ether left on it by then. It should be. You make sure it is. And you remember what to do if I don't come back by dark?"

"Yes, Eddie . . . Edward. But why wouldn't you come back?"

"I plan to be back. But you never know when one of those people out there will come nosing around. If I run into something unexpected, it might take me a little longer is all."

They rode in silence. Sari looked down at the sleeping baby. His mother, his other mother, had been right. Riding put him to sleep. He didn't know he was going to a whole new life. Just like she was. She was glad Eddie was going to let her stay with the baby and the buggy instead of going to the school with him. She didn't want to think about what he was going to do at the school. He'd told her not to think about it. She was supposed to think about having a baby and starting a new life in California. He said it would all be worth it in the end. She had to hold on to that thought.

Eddie was intent on driving, determination on his face. She knew he planned to get to Rockytop after the children went home from school, but before the teacher took off on one of her jaunts like she did most days after school. Eddie had to be finished with his business and gone before dusk when the night patrol started riding up and down the valley. Eddie had spent a lot of time figuring out what everyone in the valley did and when the best time to move around undetected was. In late afternoon the women were fixing dinner, and the men and children were doing chores. There was seldom anyone out and about then, except for the teacher. He'd even picked a Friday, Sari suspected, so that the teacher wouldn't be missed until Monday.

Sari still didn't know exactly what he was going to do with the teacher, or the hat lady, for that matter. It seemed silly to bring her along, but Eddie had insisted. Was he going to kidnap the teacher, too, and take all of them to California? Sari tried not to think about the gun he had stashed under his seat and what his plans for it were. But he *had* said he wasn't going to ask for a divorce and he *was* going to be free to marry. And he said he was going to "take care of" that cowboy. Even a dumb hillbilly like her could put two and two together and come up with murder. She tried not to think about it, like Eddie had said. She wasn't successful.

They passed Tin Can Corner without seeing anyone. When they had first arrived in the valley, they spent two days parked near the corner, hidden from sight, watching people getting their mail, until Eddie finally got to meet Sol Stonacre and talk him into letting them stay at his place. She knew he picked him because he was new to the valley. He hadn't been here last year when Eddie had done whatever it was that caused him to get injured and end up in her creek. He and Sol had hit it off right away. Of course, paying Sol helped too.

As they neared Rockytop, Eddie got more and more nervous. She could see it in the set of his jaw, the vein throbbing there, and the white knuckles that held the reins. If anything was going to go wrong, it would be along here. Someone from the valley might come along and wonder what they were doing. Finally they reached the grove of cotton-woods Eddie had found earlier and pulled the buggy in among the trees. The new leaves on the willow bushes were finally out enough that they hid the buggy from view of the road.

"Now what?" Sari asked. Her nervousness was increasing along with his. She knew the plan, but she had to ask anyway.

"Now we wait," he answered, looking at his pocket watch. "It's almost time." He took the spyglass out of their suitcase on the back seat and crawled under a bush on the side of the grove facing Rockytop. She knew he was watching to see the kids going home from school.

The baby woke up and started to get fussy. She took him on a walk along the riverbank, but that didn't settle him down. Maybe he was wet, or hungry. She checked and then clumsily changed his diaper. It had been a long time since she'd changed a diaper. She rinsed it out in the creek and hung it on a bush to dry. Back at the buggy, she had a milk bottle and some cans of Borden's in the suitcase. She didn't know if he'd ever had anything except mother's milk, but he was going to have to now. She climbed back into the buggy and fixed a bottle. The first few times she tried the canned milk, he spit out the nipple in disgust. She squeezed a little milk onto her finger and put it into his mouth. He sucked greedily. After that, he took the nipple and began drinking.

The buggy started rocking. "Eddie!" Sari called in a loud whisper. "That hat lady's done woke up. She's flopping around something fierce."

Eddie returned to the buggy, untied Lulabelle's legs, and pulled her out. She stood unsteadily, her eyes wide and frightened. Sari took the baby to where his mother could see him, so she'd know he was all right.

Eddie put his mouth close to Lulabelle's ear, causing her to cringe and try to lean away from him. He jerked on the rope that held her hands together behind her back to keep her upright. "We're going to take a little walk, darlin'," he whispered into her ear. "That means I'm going to have to leave your feet untied. But I know you're going to do just exactly what I say because, if you don't, you'll never see your baby alive again."

Lulabelle's eyes filled with tears, but she nodded her head to show she understood and agreed.

"Has all the kids done gone home?" Sari asked.

"I counted sixteen," Eddie said. "How convenient none of the little snots was absent today. I know for sure they're all gone. It's time. And this time I know it will work. Last year I came off halfcocked and really didn't plan things out. That's why I wasn't successful. And I was too angry to think straight."

"You're still angry," Sari pointed out.

"Yes, but this time it's controlled anger. This time I'm ready. And I've got surprise on my side." He started leading Lulabelle away.

Sari stared at the gun under the buggy seat. Did Eddie mean to take it with him? Should she ask him? He'd be real mad if he got up to the school and needed it and didn't have it. She was beginning to think the worst thing in the world was to have Eddie mad at you. "Ain't you forgetting something, Eddie?" Sari called. "The gun? Don't you need that?" Maybe he'd look more favorably on her if she helped him remember.

He turned and glared at her. "Not now. Don't you think I can handle two women without a gun? That's for later, when we head for New Mexico along the south road. We have to go by that piss-ant cowboy's place. I'll take care of him then. Gunshots down here would bring curious people out. Up there, they'll just think he's shooting prairie dogs."

Sari watched as they walked upstream, Eddie jerking Lulabelle by the rope every time she stumbled or hesitated. Her poor wrists would be red and raw in no time. When Sari could no longer see them, she took Junior back to the buggy to wait. She laid the blanket that had covered Lulabelle on the grass by the stream bank and put Junior on his back. He grinned and flopped his arms and legs, enjoying the warm breezes and the freedom from the blanket. It would be a joy to take care of this baby. It might even make being married to Eddie bearable. Or would it? What would happen when this baby got older, if they didn't have any more kids? Eddie wouldn't need her to take care of him when he got bigger. He wouldn't need her at all. Then what would he do? Would he start thinking about how she was the only one who knew he'd killed all them people back in Colorado? Would he want to get shut of her like he wanted to get rid of his first wife?

He'd told her to wait until almost dark. If he wasn't back by then, it meant he'd unexpectedly run into people and had to go somewhere and hide. She was to take the buggy back down to Halpern and wait for him around behind the church.

"And what should I do if you *never* come back?" she had asked.

"That's your problem," he said. She had no idea what she'd do if he never came back. All the plans, all the ideas were his. She couldn't think past driving the buggy to Halpern. But she had to. She had to think what to do. She used to know what to do. All those years raising Orville alone she knew what to do. When Eddie was lying on the river bank almost dead, she knew what to do. It was just since Eddie got better and took over everything that she didn't know. Well, Eddie wasn't with her now. She had to think. She had to decide.

CHAPTER TWENTY-FOUR

Shooting Blanks

ৎড়ঌৢৄ

Friday, May 13, 1921, Rockytop—*I know I've already written once today, diary, but I feel a need to write again, and read in my Bible some more. Now that the children are on their way home, I'll take a few minutes to do so.*

Why did I ever agree to meet Silas tonight? Nothing good can come of it. It will only make us long for what we can't have even more than we already do. It's not that I'm afraid something sinful will happen if I meet him. I know he would never force himself on me. I guess what I'm afraid of is myself—my own emotions. I'm finding it harder and harder to keep myself in check when he is around. Sometimes I think it would be better if I had never met him. Then I wouldn't know what I'm missing by not being able to return his love as he'd like. But, if I'd never met him, I would be dead at Edmund's hands by now. It was Silas who saved me last year. Well, the Lord saved me, of course, but he used Silas.

Minta opened her Bible to Psalm 34. It fell open there, in fact. She read that Psalm so often, she had most of it memorized. She especially liked the fourth verse: *I sought the Lord, and He heard me, and delivered me from all my fears.* And the fourteenth verse which had become her plan for her life: *Depart from evil and do good, seek peace and pursue it.* She had been seeking peace and pursuing it ever since she departed from Edmund's evil. Teaching was her way of doing good. Even if she never got to be with Silas, it should be enough just to have peace and do good.

So why did she feel so desolate? She continued reading to the end of the psalm: *The Lord redeemeth the soul of His servants: and none of them that trust in Him shall be desolate.* Ah! Another promise she could claim. Her grandmother had taught her to claim promises. She would trust the Lord and be a servant, serving the children and the people of the Halpern Valley. The Lord would not leave her desolate. Even if things never worked out so that she and Silas could be together, God would find another way to save her from desolation. She was sure of it.

Minta closed her books and stood up. Time to take a walk. That always lifted her spirits. Maybe she could sort out her thoughts about Silas and decide whether to meet him tonight as planned. She had just started for the door when it opened, and she saw Lulabelle standing there with her hands behind her back looking pale and frightened. Lulabelle stumbled forward as if shoved from behind, and Minta realized she *had* been. A man was coming in behind her, but Minta scarcely glanced at him, her whole attention focused on Lulabelle.

"Lulabelle, what is it?" Minta asked. "Are you all right? Is it Frank? Or the baby? What's wrong?"

Lulabelle just looked at her with sad eyes. She rolled them backwards so Minta would look at the man behind her.

She didn't recognize him—at first. But as soon as she looked into his demonic eyes, she knew. She took a step back; all the blood in her body had suddenly gone ice cold. Her thoughts went first to flight. If she could get into the bedroom and wedge the chair under the door, she might have time to escape out the window. But then, what would he do to Lulabelle? Of course, that's why he had brought Lulabelle, so Minta would do whatever he told her to. She was not going to expose Lulabelle to his violence again. She'd die first.

"What do you want, Edmund?" She tried to keep her voice steady. "Let Lulabelle go, and I'll do whatever you want. I'll go home with you, if that's what you want."

Edmund laughed his nasty laugh. "We have no home to go to, thanks to you. And, yes, you'll do whatever I tell you whether I let

Lulabelle go or not. Now, we're all going outside. Like I told your cousin, you *will* be quiet. See how quiet she is, even with her gag off? She knows what will happen to her baby if she doesn't cooperate. You wouldn't want to be responsible . . ."

"Frankie!" Minta gasped. "What have you done with him?"

"He's safe . . . for now, with my . . . accomplice. Whether he continues to be, depends on how cooperative you two are. Now, outside!"

Minta was first out the door. The bell rope was so close. If she could just give it one or two good jerks before Edmund reached her, maybe people would come in time to save Lulabelle and Frankie. Minta waited until Edmund's attention was on Lulabelle who had stumbled on the step and ran to the bell rope. She reached up and pulled, putting all her weight on the rope. Just when it came down far enough so that it should be ringing, she fell with a hard jolt onto her backside, the rope with its cut end falling useless all around her like a limp, dead snake.

Edmund was laughing. "I knew you'd try that. Fixed it before we came in."

Minta stood and brushed the dirt off her skirt. She eyed the bell. She was tall enough that, if she jumped, she could grab the bottom edge and make it ring that way. She gathered herself, bent her knees, and jumped. Edmund caught her in mid-leap, and she twisted and turned in his grasp trying to claw his eyes with her fingernails.

He laughed again as he got her arms under control. "Why weren't you ever like this in bed?" he asked. "Sleeping with you was like sleeping with a frozen fish."

"Run, Lulabelle," she gasped. But then she saw that the rope around Lulabelle's wrists was fastened to Edmund's belt.

Edmund set Minta back down on her feet and slapped her hard enough to make her fall to the ground again. He took another rope off of his waist and tied her wrists like Lulabelle's, jerking the rope so tightly she thought her wrists would be cut clean in two.

"Remember what I said about being quiet?" Edmund asked. "That's just until we get up there." He pointed to Rockytop. "Then you can make all the noise you want. No one will hear you."

"I don't want to go up there," Lulabelle's voice quivered. "I'm afraid."

"It's all right," Minta said, a desperate plan starting to take shape in her mind. "Do what he says."

"Smart woman," Edmund said. He pushed them ahead of him, poking their backs painfully whenever they didn't walk fast enough.

"We'll need our hands free when we get up higher," Minta said. "There's a place we'll need our hands to help pull ourselves up."

"We'll see about that when we get there," Edmund said.

"And watch out for rattlesnakes," Minta added.

"Is that supposed to scare me?" Edmund asked. "I've got on heavy pants and boots. Any snake we come across is going to do a lot more damage to you than to me. Now shut up until I tell you you can talk again!"

Lulabelle's tears fell fast but silently as they made their way up the sage and cactus covered slope toward the large boulders that ringed the top. Minta fought to stay dry-eyed. Her wrists felt like they were on fire, but her hands had gone numb.

They reached the last, steep, rocky climb to the top. A cleft between two boulders provided access to the relatively flat top. There was no way to continue the way they were bound unless Edmund were to carry them, and even he could see that it would be impossible for him to get through the cleft with a woman over his shoulder.

"Okay," Edmund said to Lulabelle. "You can talk now unless you say something I don't like. I'm going to untie your hands. When you're up, we'll follow. I know there's no place to run once you're up there, and this is the only way back down. You won't get past me. I checked this place out thoroughly. I know what I'm talking about."

"When were you ever up here?" Minta asked. "Last year when you were here it was in the middle of the night. Dark. You couldn't have explored up here. Besides . . ."

She'd been about to say that she and Silas had been up here last year when Edmund was burning the buildings. She remembered crouching behind the boulder and watching her cabin burn through the cleft in the rocks. The sick feeling in her stomach now was the same as she'd had then. She hadn't believed, then, that Edmund would stoop so low. Now she knew he'd stoop even lower—he was capable of anything.

"I didn't have to be up here. I could see it with my glass from across the valley. It's amazing what all I found out just by looking—and asking."

"Across the valley? Oh! Stonacres'!" It all clicked into place for Minta. Edmund had been here—for weeks—planning and scheming and tricking innocent people into helping him. It was so like what he'd do. But if he'd only seen Rockytop through a glass from across the valley, there were things he didn't know about it that she did. She had climbed it numerous times and explored all its nooks and crannies. It was her territory, not his. "You're Edward of Edward and Sarah!" Minta said. "Where's she? Does *she* have Frankie now?"

"His name's not Frankie," Edmund said. 'It's Ed. Ed Junior. I can count to nine. I know whose baby he is." He turned to Lulabelle. "Too bad we don't have time to try to make another one. But, you wouldn't live long enough to give birth."

"He's *not* yours!" Lulabelle said. "He looks just like Frank."

Edmund laughed. "Sure. Redheaded Frank and a black-haired baby. I'm surprised he didn't divorce you as soon as he saw that head coming out from between your legs. Now, get up there!" He pushed Lulabelle toward the cleft.

"I'm afraid, Minta. What if there's a snake? I don't want to put my hands up there."

"There won't be," Minta said. "The places you have to put your hands to climb are small, sharp edges where a snake wouldn't lie. Just look out where you put your feet once you get to the opening on top."

Lulabelle climbed carefully and looked back down the cleft to Minta. "No snakes," she said weakly.

It felt so good to get the rope off her wrists. Minta rubbed circulation back into her hands before she began her climb. "Don't try anything funny, Teacher," Edmund said. "Or I'll teach you a thing or two. The last things you ever learn, in fact."

Minta turned in mid-climb and looked back down at him. "No, that's not true, Edmund. Once I'm with the Lord I will continue to learn. I'll learn everything I've ever wanted to know. I'm looking forward to it."

"Good," Edmund said. "You'll get your wish—very, very soon. You'll even get to go to your reward with your new boyfriend. He's next on my list."

Minta gasped. "You have no cause to hurt Silas," she exclaimed. "He's *not* my boyfriend and never has been."

"How quickly you jump to his defense. Don't pretend with me. I know you for the liar you are. Just remember it was your lies that caused all this. You have no one to blame but yourself."

Minta gritted her teeth. How like Edmund to blame others for his actions. She turned and finished climbing up to Lulabelle. She looked down at Edmund. "So, if you're going to kill us anyway, why should we continue to cooperate with you?" she asked.

"Because I have the baby under my control. His only chance of making it to his first birthday is if his mother and her cousin do exactly as I say, and I return to Sarah before dark. You won't be around to celebrate his birthday with him, but you can go to that Maker you're so anxious to meet with the knowledge you saved his life."

"Sarah wouldn't kill a baby," Minta said. She'd never met Sarah, but she couldn't imagine any woman capable of killing a baby.

"Do you want to bet his life on that?" Edmund asked. His eyes bored into her. "What would she do without me to take care of her and the baby? She'll dump him in the creek as fast as she can and make tracks out of here if I don't return to her. She doesn't have your misplaced sense of responsibility. She'll take care of herself and no one else."

Lulabelle fell to the ground, sobbing. "Don't argue with him, Minta. Do whatever he says. It doesn't matter what happens to us. All that matters now is Frankie."

Edmund climbed quickly up through the cleft and stood with his back to it. Minta helped Lulabelle up, and they moved further back away from him toward the low rocks on the back side. "Don't look down," Minta whispered to Lulabelle. "Move as far as you can toward that flat rock over there."

"What are you whispering about?" Edmund asked. "Oh well, it doesn't matter. This is where it ends. I wonder how long it will take them to find your bodies? I suppose the vultures will give you away eventually, but your friends won't even start looking until Monday when you don't show up for school."

"People are looking for *me* right now!" Lulabelle said. "When I didn't come downstairs after Frankie's nap time, Frank would have started looking for us."

"So, they'll look in and around Liberty. They won't have any reason to look out here."

"Yes, they will. Frank will wonder if I decided to come see Minta, and he'll look out here."

"Then I guess we'd better make this quick," Edmund said. He stretched a length of rope between his hands. "This will work on your pretty little throat. I'd like to do you first so my wife could watch you suffer, but she'd come after me with her claws. She's not nearly as cooperative as you are. It's time to get her out of the way." He turned toward Minta, loosening and then jerking the rope so it made loud snapping sounds as he approached her.

"Promise me you won't hurt my baby," Lulabelle sobbed.

"I told you, I'm going to raise *my* son up right. He'll be a *real* man someday—not a wimpy dry goods peddler."

"He's not your son," Minta said quietly, stepping backwards and up a foot onto the flat rock until she could feel the edge of the drop-off behind her through her soles. "You're impotent—unable to father children. Doc Watters told me when you made me go see him. Remember when you had mumps as a teenager? The doctor said that killed all your sperm. He said you're . . . you're shooting blanks." She didn't even remember where she had heard such a crude term, but knew the effect it would have on Edmund.

She watched his face go from red to chalk white, back to red. "Liar!" he screamed as he dropped the rope and lunged for her, his carefully thought-out plan forgotten. She turned her head slightly and in her peripheral vision could see the drop-off behind her. It would be so easy to just lean back and fall into oblivion. Much easier than facing Edmund. She felt slightly dizzy, like she had when she saw the ground just before she fell out of the tree that time she broke her arm.

That had been the last time Lulabelle beat her at Indian wrestling. After Minta's arm healed and she could use it again, she began challenging the boys at school to Indian wrestle. At first they always won. But she kept at it, getting stronger and stronger, and, more importantly, learning their tricks. Like grabbing your opponent's arm sooner than expected, catching him off balance.

As Edmund reached for her throat, she grabbed his forearm and pulled. She fell forward and to the side as his momentum and her pull propelled him past her—and over the edge. He didn't cry out. The only sound was a sickening thud followed by the rattle of small rocks that had been dislodged bouncing downhill.

Minta didn't want to look, but she had to know. She crawled back to the edge and looked down on the talus slope at the base of the cliff. Edmund's limbs were splayed at unnatural angles, making him look like a spider that had been stepped on. A red spot on the rocks under his head widened as she watched. She forced her eyes to stay on him for what seemed a long time. He didn't move. She crawled back to Lulabelle who was sobbing uncontrollably.

"He's dead," Minta said flatly. When Lulabelle didn't respond, she asked, "Are you all right?"

"I'm . . . I'm all right," Lulabelle sobbed. "But now we don't know where Frankie is! What if that woman left him somewhere all alone? What if she *does* throw him in the creek? It will be dark soon. We have to find him!" She stumbled to her feet and toward the cleft.

"Slow down, Lulabelle," Minta shouted. "If you break your neck getting down, it won't do him any good. I'm sure he's all right. That woman will take care of him."

"What if she already took off with him? She has a horse and buggy. And, and a gun. I saw it under the seat when I woke up. What if he told her to kill Frankie if he doesn't come back? Oh, why did you kill Edmund before we got Frankie back?"

"Lulabelle! Do you think I had a choice? If I hadn't done something right then, we'd both be dead. And Frankie would be facing life with Edmund. That's worse than being dead. You're not thinking straight."

Any further talking was precluded by their frantic, headlong flight down the hill. When they got to the school, Minta jumped for the bell and caught the edge of it in her hands. She let go as she fell back to earth, and it clanged several times. She jumped again. And again. When she saw the dust trails of people coming, she fell to the ground in an exhausted heap, oblivious to Lulabelle's wailing.

CHAPTER TWENTY-FIVE

Forgive Us Our Trespasses

༄

Monday, May 16, 1921, Rockytop—*Fred asked if I wanted to cancel school for a few days, but I refused. My problems with Edmund caused a wreck at the end of last school year. I'm determined they won't this year. The children need the normalcy of the end of school activities as planned.*

The Stonacres were the last to arrive in response to the bell. I'm surprised they came at all. Ruby explained to Claudia that the children insisted they come, even threatening to run all the way by themselves if their parents didn't hitch up the wagon. Dennis told them, "That bell means the teacher's hurt and is gonna be et up by a big wolf unless we go help her." How close to right he was!

Sol was livid when he found out how Edmund had lied to him and used him. Sol kept assuring everyone that he never would have let those people stay at his place if he'd known. I guess he's starting to care what the neighbors think about him.

I can hardly bear to think past the last day of school. I don't know what to do about next year. I don't think I can stand to live in the shadow of Rockytop. The scar from last year's fire haunted me all this year. Now, living at the bottom of Rockytop, the scene of . . .

Minta put down her pen and looked out her window—the one that faced the valley, not the one that faced Rockytop. As if celebrating a world without Edmund, it had rained most of the weekend—a slow, gentle rain—just what they needed. Already the pastures had greened up and Halpern Creek gurgled happily. Would she be able to be happy here again? She had taken a life. Even if she escaped the shadow of Rockytop, she would never escape that fact. She could ask for forgiveness and know it was granted, but she would have a much harder time forgiving herself—or Edmund. How could she expect to receive forgiveness if she couldn't grant it?

She remembered lying on the ground after ringing the bell for help. No one could get her to get up for a long time. Lulabelle had been hysterical, and the first women to arrive, Claudia and Rachel, spent their time calming her down so that she could tell them what had happened and the route she and Edmund had taken to get to Rockytop. Once it was clear they'd left Frankie and Sarah in a grove of cottonwoods and walked upstream, Lulabelle wanted to go running headlong downstream to find Frankie herself. Minta roused herself enough to warn the others that Sarah had a gun. At that, Fred and Paulo took up their rifles and started downstream, with Richard escorting Lulabelle behind them.

When they got to the cottonwood grove, the horse, buggy, and people were gone. Lulabelle became hysterical again, but they found buggy tracks heading downstream and started following them. Halfway to Halpern they met Reverend MacIntosch and Ben Griffith riding toward them. Apparently, Sarah had walked into the Halpern church, handed Frankie to Mrs. MacIntosch who was inside cleaning, said, "Bad stuff is goin' on at that school up there where them rocks is," jumped back in the buggy, and took off. Reverend MacIntosch had looked up Ben, and they started toward Rockytop to see what was happening.

Ernst had ridden to town to get Frank and the sheriff as soon as he found out what happened. Lulabelle had been right about Frank deciding to search for her at Rockytop. They were already on their way there, along with Matthew Post, when Richard met them on the back trail.

Several of the men took Fred's wagon around back of Rockytop as far as it would go and then hiked in to the body. They laid it on a blanket and carried it to the wagon to wait for transport to town with the sheriff. When they got back to the school, it was Silas who finally got Minta to sit up, and then stand and go inside. He helped her lie down on her bed and shooed away the people who tried to come in to talk to her.

"I have to talk to the sheriff, Silas," she said. But she didn't get up.

"You will. There's no hurry. First, I have to make sure you're all right." He felt her limbs, one by one, as if he expected them to be broken.

"I didn't break my arm this time," she mumbled as he went into the schoolroom, dipped his handkerchief in the hand-washing bucket, and came back to gently wipe away the dust and blood from her face and hands. Her wrists stung as he cleaned the rope burns.

"I wish he wasn't already dead," Silas said as he cleaned her bruised face, "so I could kill him myself."

"No you don't," Minta said. "Killing someone is awful. Go get the sheriff, I have to tell him. . ."

"All in good time, Minta. Sit up. There. You're looking more presentable. How do you feel?"

"Numb," she said, shivering. He took off his jacket and placed it around her shoulders.

When the search party came back after retrieving Frankie from the church, Lulabelle came to the bedroom door with the baby. "Minta, Frank wants to take us home. It will be dark soon, and he wants me to see the doctor. I can't convince him I'm all right, this time."

Minta stood and walked shakily over to Frankie who lay peacefully in Lulabelle's arms. She kissed the top of his head, then looked up into Lulabelle's exhausted eyes. "I'm so sorry, Lulabelle. This was all my fault."

"Don't start that again, Minta," Silas ordered. "It's *not* your fault. And the one whose fault it is won't be bothering either of you ever again."

Frank came in then and insisted his wife and baby leave with him. The sheriff was right behind him. Minta asked Silas to leave while she talked to Mo. She told him exactly what had happened, leaving nothing out, excusing nothing. "So, I grabbed his arm and pulled him over the edge," she finished.

The sheriff had been making notes in a small notebook he carried. "Yes, I understand, Minta. Edmund tripped and fell over the edge."

"No, Moses. I caused him to fall."

"Impossible to tell, I imagine. It happened so fast. His speed and weight probably carried him over the edge. It was just an accident."

"It was *not* an accident. I planned it, and I did it. I think that's called premeditation. I meditated about it all the way up Rockytop."

"Well, not legally. See, I got to fill out my report based on what I understand to have happened, and I understand that he was running toward you, didn't know the drop-off was there, couldn't stop himself in time, and went over the edge." He flipped the notebook shut.

"But . . ."

"There's not a judge or jury in this state that would fault you for what you did. And I know Judge Vieland. I'll be in trouble for wasting the court's time if I bring you up on charges, seeing as how it was self-defense and all. Now, I've got to see if we can catch up to that woman accomplice."

"I doubt she was an accomplice. Oh, she helped him. But he forced her to—somehow. He's . . . was . . . very good at forcing people to do things."

So far, no sign of the woman, Sarah, or the buggy had been found. In some ways, Minta hoped she would make her escape. Sarah had run from Edmund, just as Minta had. She'd even stolen a horse and buggy from him, too. She wouldn't know that Edmund was now dead, and she would have to change her name and start a new life just as Minta had done. That alone was punishment enough.

Minta forced her mind back to the present. She didn't have time to sit around wondering what had happened to that woman. The children would be here soon. This would be as normal a school day as possible for them; she'd see to that.

She expected questions from the children about what had happened, but none of them said a word. Their parents must have instructed them not to. Michael brought a new length of rope to school, and Robert, the best climber, shinnied up the pole to attach it to the bell. Then he wrapped a rag around the clapper so it wouldn't ring, and Michael tried the rope to make sure it pulled the bell properly and didn't come undone. "Thank you, boys," Minta said.

"Father said this bell paid for itself several times this year," Robert said. "'Best investment the school board ever made', he said."

"Remember when Dennis rang the bell?" Gunny asked. "A lot sure has happened since then."

"Yes," Minta replied. "And now he and all of you know why you should never cry wolf."

"I still don't get what wolves has to do with it," Judy said.

"I think the wolf runned away," Dennis informed her. "Probably the bell done scared him off."

"You'll learn about analogies in eighth grade," Angus said when the laughter died down.

"Speaking of eighth grade," Minta said, "we'd better go in now. End of school tests are coming up soon. Today we'll review. I want you to ask about anything you don't understand even if it's something we worked on a long time ago—even if it's something you learned and then forgot. I won't get mad at you for forgetting."

"We know, Miss Mayfield," Mary said. "You never get mad about stuff like that—just really bad things."

Minta wished Mary's statement were true. She thought about all the times she'd been cranky with the children for no good reason. It's a good thing they were so forgiving. Now, would she be able to follow their example?

❖·❖·❖

After school, Matthew Post and Moses Upton came knocking. She let them in and offered to make coffee.

"No thank you," the sheriff said. "We came on business. I called the law in Indiana and they got hold of Edmund's brother like you said. He said he didn't want the body shipped back there. His exact words were, 'His poor wife can do whatever she wants with the sorry bas . . . son of a gun.'"

"We know you don't want to have to deal with this, Minta. Would you like me to make some sort of funeral arrangements?" Matthew asked.

"Ask me, you should just throw him in the Liberty River and let New Mexico figure out what to do with his bones when they get there," Mo said.

"No," Minta said. "It's my responsibility to see he gets a proper burial."

"Would you like me to help you make arrangements with the cemetery in Halpern, or maybe the one in Liberty?" Matthew asked.

"No! Neither! They're too close," Minta said. "How about Durango? Could we bury him there?"

"I'm sure we can. I'll make all the arrangements. Do you want a church service?"

"No. Just a graveside service. I'm sure Reverend MacIntosch would say something if I ask him."

"I'll ask him on the way back to town," Matthew offered. "I assume you want it done as soon as possible?"

"Yes, please," Minta said.

"Will you be wanting to attend?" Matthew asked. "You don't have to."

"Of course I do. I must."

"If you're worried about what people might think . . ."

"No, it's not that. I need to attend. For me. For my peace of mind."

"I can see why you'd want to make sure he's planted six feet under," Mo said. "I guarantee he won't be coming back from the dead this time around."

"I don't think that's what she meant," Matthew said as they turned to go. "I'll let you know as soon as I've made arrangements," he called back to Minta.

So it was that they did call off school for a day—the day she went to Durango to see the end of her ill-fated marriage. Minta expected to have only the company of the Posts and Reverend MacIntosch, but to her surprise, nearly all the adults from Rockytop were there, a solid line of support standing with her. Sophie had stayed behind to watch the children with the help of Clara and Mary, and Lulabelle and Frank chose not to attend. They agreed with the sheriff about the proper disposal of the body.

The cemetery was on a hill overlooking the Animas River. Blooming trees scented the May air with the hint of fruit to come. It was a day filled with the promise of new beginnings.

Silas stood at her side until Reverend MacIntosch finished praying and everyone turned to leave. She looked down into the freshly dug grave and at the box that held her worst memories and most frightening nightmares. If only it were as easy to get rid of them as it was going to be to shovel the dirt over the box and get rid of the earthly remains. She dabbed at her eyes with her handkerchief.

"He's not worth your tears, Minta," Silas said.

"I'm not crying for him. I'm crying for all I've lost. Most of all my innocence."

"How about we start thinking about what all you can now gain?" Silas asked. He took her arm and led her away from the grave.

"I can't. Not yet, anyway. I'm sorry, Silas. I know you thought that now . . . but it's not that simple. Not that easy. I need some time."

Silas frowned in confusion. Several times he started to say something and then stopped. When they reached Matthew's buggy, he helped her in. She looked down at him. She wanted to say something to ease the pain in his eyes but couldn't think of anything else to say. Her own pain was too fresh. They looked at each other for a long time.

Finally he just said, "I guess I can wait. I'm getting real good at it."

CHAPTER TWENTY-SIX

Mountains and Molehills

༈

Friday, May 27, 1921, Rockytop—*The last day. Again. I know now what the term "bittersweet" means. I am so happy this school year is over and so sad that I will never again have this exact same combination of students. Angus passed the Eighth Grade Exam, and I will be attending his graduation in Liberty tomorrow. There were almost forty students in the Liberty School for the test, more people his age than he'd ever seen in one place before. But he did fine. I'm so proud of him. After I left him at the school to take the test, I walked over to the jail to talk to Mo. They still haven't found Edmund's accomplice, Sarah. They don't even know her last name or have a picture to put on a wanted poster. Mo said, "I 'spect if she wants to stay hid, she will. At least she returned the baby in good shape." Lulabelle is still very angry at her. I'm not. I know what she must have had to endure at Edmund's hands. At least I can forgive her.*

It still scares me to think what almost happened. Lulabelle and I could be dead, Silas murdered, too. Even when they found our bodies, they would think Frankie had been with Lulabelle and his body carried off by predators. Instead, he would be facing a miserable childhood as Edmund's son. They would suspect Edmund in our deaths, of course, and look for him. But no one knew how much his appearance was altered, and they'd be looking for a single man, not a man, woman, and baby. He came so close to having his way!

Maybe I can undo at least some of the wrongs Edmund perpetrated by helping Lulabelle recover—again. But what, if anything, can undo the wrongs done to me? "Now, don't go feeling sorry for yourself, Missy." I can hear Grandmother say. "Lots

༈ 186 ༈

of people in the world are worse off than you. You could be a poor child working in a mine in Wales." That's what she always said when I complained about having to do my chores. I don't know where she got the idea there were mines employing children in Wales, but it was one of her favorite sayings.

I get such comfort from my memories of my grandmother. Maybe it's time to go back to my own parents. There's nothing to stop me now. Well, nothing but—Silas. I'm just not sure I'd make him or anyone a good wife now. First I couldn't marry him because I was married. Then, because I didn't know if Edmund were alive or dead. Now, I can't saddle him with a self-pitying murderer for a wife. He deserves better.

Minta and Silas sat together to watch the Rockytop Rattlers take on the Halpern Coyotes in the championship game. Before the game, the children, each one shaking a rattlesnake rattle, sang their new fight song to the delight of the crowd and the disgust of the Halpern bunch who started to boo until their teacher, Ben Griffith, stood and fixed them with a stern glare. Matthew made a point of telling her students how much he admired their school spirit. Then he turned to her. "And I know to whom the credit goes, Minta. I've never seen a group of kids who get along so well with each other."

She almost choked, thinking of all the problems they had had during most of the school year. Good thing Matthew hadn't dropped in unexpectedly. "Don't give me the credit," she said. "They have the example set by their parents. Everyone in the valley gets along, now."

"Even with Sol Stonacre?" Matthew asked.

"Yes, he and Fred have become good friends."

"I figured if anyone could talk some sense into him, it would be Fred. And I do give you the credit for goading Fred into making the effort. It's a lot easier to mind your own business, and most of us males prefer to do that. Well, they're about to start. I'll let you and Silas enjoy the game. I need to find Miriam."

Last year Minta had been so involved in the game she hadn't been aware of who was around her. This year it was Silas who was enthralled. "Look at that catch!" he yelled when Robert came down with a particularly difficult ball. Robert *had* improved. If he'd been able to jump and catch like that last year, they would have won the game.

It was still a close game. As predicted, the littlest ones—Beth, Dale, and Gina—made most of their outs, and Michael, Solly, and Angus made most of their runs. The few surprises were Dennis, who got a double, and Judy, who hit a ball hard enough to bring Gunny in from third, even though she got put out at first.

Before Minta realized what had happened, Silas jumped to his feet, yelling and applauding. Rockytop had won, nine to eight. As Minta was taking in that fact, she felt a tap on her shoulder. She turned to see Ben Griffith. "Congratulations, Minta," he said. "Your group did a fine job this year. I'm glad we finally have another teacher around here who takes softball seriously."

"Are you, Ben?" she asked.

"Well, almost," he said. "It would have been better if *we* won. But we'll get you next year."

"We'll just see about that," Silas said. "I'm going to coach the team next year, so you'd better start your team practicing this summer. Never mind, it's already too late for you," he teased.

"Them's fighting words." Ben laughed as he walked away. "Oh, and the rattles. Nice touch. I can already see my bunch wanting to make up a song now. Hope the little woman will help me with that! I have no abilities that way at all."

Silas and Minta congratulated each child and listened to their verbal replay of the most exciting parts of the game until their parents came looking for them to start home.

"I have something for you, Fred," Minta said when he came to collect his brood. "I'll get it out of my purse." She handed him the register for the year, which she had finished filling out the night before.

"Oh, thanks," Fred said. "But there's no hurry on this. I could get it from you any time this summer."

"I'm not sure where I'll be," Minta said. "Just in case I don't see you again. Soon, I mean," she added when he looked up in alarm. He'd been flipping through the pages, probably seeing if she'd filled out everything.

"I see you used corporal punishment once," he said. "Funny, I don't remember the kids telling me about it. That's usually something they tell. Doesn't say who, though."

"No. It only asks for a number, not a name."

"And . . ." Fred waited.

"And, that's all I'm going to say about it."

"Which means it was one of mine," Fred said.

"Think what you like," Minta replied.

"Boy, she's gotten feisty this year," Fred said to Silas.

"I think she must have been born that way," Silas answered.

After Fred left, Silas and Minta walked back toward their mounts. "Michael," Silas said.

"What?"

"I'll bet it was Michael. At first I thought probably Solly, but then I realized Michael was the one most likely to get under your skin."

"You know me too well," Minta said.

"I'd like to know you a lot better. Have you thought about . . . you know . . our future? I said I'd wait until you're ready, and I will, but I'd sure like to get started on it."

"Of course, I've thought about it. It's almost all I think about," she said.

Silas hadn't let a day go by since Edmund's death without visiting her and asking her to marry him. She figured he thought eventually he'd wear her down. She still hadn't decided what would be best. She knew what she *wanted* to do, but would it be fair to Silas?

"I don't think I'd make a good wife for you, Silas. I've killed a man, and I can't forget that. It will weigh on my mind, and . . ."

"I don't expect you to forget it. I expect you to get past it, with my help."

"I can't Silas. It's not that easy. No one understands how I feel. I *killed* someone!"

"Excuse me, Minta, but if *anyone* can understand how you feel, it's me. Did you forget?"

"Oh, I'm sorry Silas. I did forget you killed a man, too. But you didn't mean to. I *meant* to."

"I may not have meant to, but I was just as guilty. More so. You were defending yourself and your cousin. I was just being stupid. If I hadn't got drunk and got in a situation with other dumb guys and guns . . . Don't you think it weighs on my mind, too?"

"I don't know. It hasn't seemed like it."

"Well, it does. But not as much as it used to. I just don't go around talking about it. I know I'll never forget it, and I probably shouldn't. But it gets easier to think about, over time. That's what I meant about getting past it. I can help you. You can help me. We can get past it together."

"Just two lonely desperadoes?" She smiled sadly at him.

"If that's how you want to think of it. But I hope there's more than two of us eventually."

Minta's heart did a little flip-flop at the thought of more little Silases. Her children. She was afraid to get her hopes up again that she could have a normal life, marriage, children. They rode in silence until Rockytop came into view. Minta reined in her horse and sat staring at Rockytop. It was the first time she'd allowed herself to really look at it since that awful Friday the Thirteenth.

'What do you see?" Silas asked.

"Just a small mountain. One I need to make a molehill of." She dismounted.

"What are you talking about?" Silas asked, taking his place beside her. They let the horses wander toward the creek and the green grass there.

"Grandmother always told me not to make mountains out of molehills. I need to turn it around and make a molehill out of Rockytop. Otherwise, I'm always going to be afraid to be too close to it."

"Would it help you to go back up there with me?"

"Maybe sometime. Grandmother also said it was best to face your fears. But not today. Not until the wind and rain have done their work and erased all signs of what happened there, made it like a fresh, clean blackboard. Next fall—when it's time to start a new school year. Most people think spring is the time for new beginnings, but I know that it's really fall. Fall is when we start all over."

"We? You and me, Minta? Do you think we could start over as soon as this fall? Could you start school as Mrs. Calhoun instead of Miss Mayfield?"

"No. I'd need to *start* as Miss Mayfield. I owe my students and the families here at least one more year. I'd like to give them a school year that didn't end with their teacher almost murdered. All that turmoil isn't good for the children."

"Then, after you do that, could you marry me, Minta?"

"I think so, Silas. I think I could—if you still want to by then. I want you to be very sure that marrying me is what you really want."

"I've never been more sure of anything. But what about you? What do *you* want? Do you love me as much as I love you? I've been hoping . . . waiting to hear you say it."

Minta looked back up at Rockytop. The setting sun was hitting the rocks on top, highlighting them. She remembered how beautiful it could be up there. And how beautiful it was down here. And how much she wanted to stay. And how much she loved Silas.

"Yes, Silas. I love you. I wasn't free to say it before. Now I can. I may never stop saying it. I love you, I love you, I lo . . ."

But Minta did have to stop saying it, because Silas' mouth covered hers.

About the Author

❧

Jean Campion is a Colorado native who grew up in a family of educators, hearing the tales of one-room schools and the people who taught at them. She now lives in a rural area where she participated in a local history project, which collected first-person accounts of one-room schools in southwest La Plata County. That research became the impetus for *Minta Forever* and its sequel, *Return to Rockytop*. She taught writing at Fort Lewis College in Durango, Colorado, for fifteen years as well as teaching in K-12 classrooms and helping home school several children. She has been married to her high school sweetheart for over forty years, and they have three grown children and one new grandson.